VIRAGO
MODERN CLASSICS
109

Barbara Comyns

Born in 1909 at Bidford-on-Avon, Barbara Comyns was educated
mainly by governesses until she went to art schools in Stratford-
upon-Avon and London. She started writing fiction at the age of
ten and her first novel, *Sisters by a River*, was published in 1947. She
also worked in an advertising agency, a typewriting bureau, dealt in
old cars and antique furniture, bred poodles, converted and let flats,
and exhibited pictures in The London Group. She was married first
in 1931, to an artist, and for the second time in 1945. With her
second husband she lived in Spain for eighteen years. She died in
1992.

Books by Barbara Comyns

Sisters by a River

Our Spoons Came from Woolworths

Who Was Changed and Who Was Dead

The Vet's Daughter

Out of the Red and into the Blue

The Skin Chairs

Birds in Tiny Cages

A Touch of Mistletoe

The Juniper Tree

Mr Fox

The House of Dolls

OUR SPOONS
CAME FROM
WOOLWORTHS

Barbara Comyns

Introduced by Maggie O'Farrell

virago

*The only things that are true in this story are the wedding and
Chapters 10, 11 and 12 and the poverty.*

VIRAGO

This edition published by Virago Press in 2013

7 9 10 8 6

Published in paperback by Virago Press Limited in 1983
First published in Great Britain by Eyre & Spottiswode 1950

A CIP catalogue record for this book
is available from the British Library.

ISBN 978-1-84408-927-7

Typeset in Goudy by M Rules
Printed and bound in Great Britain by
Clays Ltd, St Ives plc

Papers used by Virago are from well-managed forests
and other responsible sources.

MIX
Paper from
responsible sources
FSC® C104740

Virago Press
An imprint of
Little, Brown Book Group
Carmelite House
50 Victoria Embankment
London EC4Y 0DZ

An Hachette UK Company
www.hachette.co.uk

www.virago.co.uk

INTRODUCTION

I first encountered *Our Spoons Came from Woolworths* in a second-hand bookshop in Lyme Regis. Spotting the familiar dark green spine in among a row of mildewed paperbacks, I pulled it out. I had never read any Barbara Comyns; the name was unfamiliar to me and the title name-checked a shop synonymous with the taste of slightly stale pick 'n' mix. But as I have a habit of buying up any Virago Modern Classics I don't already own, I decided to override these misgivings and make the purchase.

It would prove to be the best fifty pence I ever spent. I began to flick through the pages as I walked away from the shop. Just five minutes later, I was so engrossed that I had to stop and sit down on a bench on the Cobb; I didn't make it back to the holiday flat for some time. When I finished the novel, I resolved not only to track down all her other books but to find out as much as I could about Barbara Comyns.

My research yielded stories of a life defined by both variety and instability – which is wholly unsurprising once you've read her novels. She was born in 1909 in a Warwickshire village, one of six children. Her father, the managing director of a chemicals firm, was by her own description 'an impatient, violent man, alternatively spoiling and frightening us'. Her mother was a childlike invalid, lavishing more attention on her pet monkey than on her children. She went deaf at twenty-five, and Barbara and her siblings had to communicate with her 'in deaf and dumb language on our hands'. The children seem to have spent most of their time in boats: 'It is extraordinary,' Comyns remarked, 'that none of us was drowned because only two of us could swim.'

She began to write and illustrate stories at the age of ten: 'I don't know which I enjoyed most, the writing or drawing.' By her late teens, she was living alone in a bedsit in London. At twenty-one, she married fellow artist John Pemberton; 'after two children and many troubles, we parted more or less amicably'. Photographs show her as pale-skinned and large-eyed, with the expressive, ethereal beauty of a silent movie star. She supported herself by working as an artists' model, by converting old houses into flats, selling vintage cars, and breeding poodles, but 'all the time [she] was writing'. Her first novel, *Sisters by a River*, was published in 1947, after being serialised under the unprophetic subtitle 'The Novel Nobody Will Publish'. *Our Spoons Came from Woolworths* followed in 1950.

I defy anyone to read the opening twenty or so pages of *Our Spoons Came from Woolworths* and not to be drawn in, just as I was that day on the windy Cobb. It is a novel much dependent on voice and this one is engagingly unguarded and instantly intriguing: within the first chapter, Sophia has disclosed that she has met a man called Charles on a train, that they were both carrying artists' portfolios; they decide to get married but are too shy to ring the bell at the church door.

They go to view a flat in Haverstock Hill, whereupon the landlady's medium sister promptly falls into a trance and switches into the voice of a Chinese man called Mr Hi Wu, telling them that they are 'so lucky to be offered such a beautiful flat for only twenty-five shillings a week'.

It's safe to say that this is a novel in which you are never quite sure what will happen next. Over the following pages, we hear of the young couple's defiant marriage – against Charles's family's wishes – and of Sophia's habit of carrying about her pet newt and giving him swims in water jugs. The newt is even present at the wedding, 'in [her] pocket, as a kind of page', and as the ceremony takes place, birds are singing from the church's rafters, and someone in the congregation is shouting out to ask if Sophia would like a kitten.

So far, so charming and madcap. But any astute reader of fiction will know that if a couple are happy and in love at the start of a novel then the situation can only turn sour. Such is the way of narrative. A matter of weeks into the marriage, Charles is horrified and appalled to learn that Sophia is pregnant: '[He] made me feel,' Sophia says, 'I had betrayed him in some way.' He refuses to give up his life as a struggling painter and Sophia, purely on account of her pregnancy, is let go from her job, thereby losing the only income they have. Their bohemian idyll rapidly descends into a terrifyingly precarious existence, staked out by poverty and malnutrition.

Our Spoons Came from Woolworths is far from what it might at first appear – a comic novel about love's trials and tribulations. It is instead an account of a marriage dismantled by poverty. It charts the erosion of a woman's spirit by her husband's vain and casual cruelty. By the final pages, the reader is left in a state of suspended shock that such things could ever happen.

Comyns builds up to the novel's central, tragic climax with artful clarity; much of its impact lies in the disparity between tone and content. *Our Spoons Came from Woolworths* is a stream of digressive, conversational confidences and asides – airy, witty and yet concealing great pain. Sophia relates the most dreadful events in the same light tone that she deploys for the adventure of the wedding, which proves to be an upsettingly effective device. The reader turns the pages, lulled by the rhythms of Sophia's spirited recall into thinking she is about to be treated to another account of painting furniture sea green or a visit to an amusingly lazy sculptor, only to realise with horror that what she is faced with is the death of an infant.

Words such as 'unique' and 'original' are overused in describing prose style but it's tempting to reach for them when trying to convey what is so compelling about Barbara Comyns. Quite simply, she writes like no one else. With other authors you are able to discern the shadows of literary predecessors hovering over the page; with Comyns, you have the distinct impression that she is writing straight from her own subconscious, that her work is untrammelled by influence.

It's unsurprising, then, to learn that the events of *Our Spoons Came from Woolworths* run close to those of Comyns' own life, so much so that Comyns' daughter, on reading the manuscript, was moved to protest, 'But you've killed me!' My relief at coming across that anecdote was overwhelming as so much of the novel has the ring of truth to it and even the possibility that the death of the baby might have come from experience was too much to bear.

Our Spoons Came from Woolworths brings to life for us the lost world of interwar bohemian London, as well as illustrating just how badly Britain needed the Beveridge Report. That Sophia survives such hardship and tragedy is a testament to her will and indomitable brio. She is a heroine in every sense – and one you will never forget.

Maggie O'Farrell, 2012

1

I told Helen my story and she went home and cried. In the evening her husband came to see me and brought some strawberries; he mended my bicycle, too, and was kind, but he needn't have been, because it all happened eight years ago, and I'm not unhappy now. I hardly dare admit it, even touching wood, but I'm so happy that when I wake in the morning I can't believe it's true. I seldom think of the time when I was called Sophia Fairclough; I try to keep it pushed right at the back of my mind. I can't quite forget it because of Sandro, and often I find myself regretting lovely little Fanny. I wish I hadn't told Helen so much; it's brought everything back in a vivid flash. I can see Charles's white pointed face, and hear his husky nervous voice. I keep remembering things all the time.

We met for the first time on a railway journey. We were both carrying portfolios; that is what started us talking to each other. The next day Charles 'phoned me at the studio where I worked, and we met every day after that. The sun seemed to shine perpetually that summer, the days were all shimmering and beautiful. It never rained, yet everything remained fresh and green, even in London. The summers used to be like that when I was a child, and in the winters there was always deep snow or hard frost. The weather has grown all half-hearted now; soon we won't be able to tell the change in the seasons except by the fall of the leaf, like it says in the Holy Bible, and that will be the end of the world; at least I think it says that.

Charles and I were both twenty when we met, and as soon as we were twenty-one we decided to get married secretly. There was a church next door to the house where I had a bed-sitting-room, so we went there to ask the priest to put the banns up. We dared not ring the bell at first, we felt too shy. Charles said they would ask us in and give us a glass of sherry and some funeral biscuits. We stood on the doorstep rehearsing what to say and the priest must have heard us, because he suddenly opened the door although we hadn't rung the bell. He took one look at us with his deepset eyes and said 'Banns' in a shouting kind of voice. He asked us some questions and wrote down the answers in a black notebook, and said if we had an organ it would cost extra, and confetti cost extra, too, because of all the mess it made, so we said we could do without both those things, and he shut the door again. We went back to my bed-sitting-room and planned how we would spend the ten pounds Charles had just received for painting a screen with Victorian women creeping about. He painted it for one of his Aunt Emma's friends, and he was offended afterwards because it was put in the maid's bedroom, but we were glad of the ten pounds because that was all we had to spend on our entire home.

A few days after we had arranged about the banns we had dinner with a spiritualist friend of ours, and after we had drunk a little wine confided our marriage plans to her. She was highly delighted to be involved in a secret wedding, and when we told her we only had ten pounds to furnish our home she gave us a cheque for another ten pounds to go with it; she also said she knew someone who had a flat to let on Haverstock Hill. Not satisfied with all this help, she offered to give us a little reception at her flat after the wedding.

The next free afternoon we had, we went to the address in Haverstock Hill she had given us. A woman with very fuzzy black hair came to the door. She had a huge silver belt round her waist, and arty, messy clothes. She kept saying 'GER-G E R' after every few words, rather like a giant cat purring. She showed us the flat, which consisted of a large basement room with an old-fashioned dresser, and a small kitchen and use of bath and lav. When we had seen it she said we had better meet her sister 'GER-G E R', so we went upstairs and met the sister, who had even more fuzzy hair, but it was fair, and her eyes were round and blue and her face like a melting strawberry ice cream, rather a cheap one, and I expect her body was like that, too, only it was mostly covered in mauve velvet. She spoke to us a little and said we were little love-birds looking for a nest. She made us feel all awful inside. Then she suddenly went into a trance. We thought she was dying, but her sister explained she was a medium and governed by a Chinese spirit called Mr Hi Wu. Then Mr Hi Wu spoke to us in very broken English and told us we were so lucky to be offered such a beautiful flat for only twenty-five shillings a week; it was worth at least thirty-five. So when she had recovered we said we would have the flat, and left the first week's rent as deposit.

After this we had a frantic time shopping; we did most of it in Chalk Farm Road, N.W. We bought a massive oval table for

3

seven-and-six, and chairs for one-and-six. A carpenter made us some little stools because I like sitting on stools better than anything else. We painted all our furniture duck-egg green with a dash of sea green; we had the paint specially mixed for us. We found the rugs rather expensive; we had to have two and they were a pound each. The sheets and blankets were a great worry, too. We had to get the divan on hire purchase and for months after were having trouble over it; we nearly lost it several times, but after two years it really belonged to us, and they sent us a large and legal paper to say it did.

We redecorated the flat ourselves. Because the room was rather dark we painted the walls a kind of stippled yellow; lots of black hairs from the brush got mixed with the paint, but they looked as if they were meant to be there almost.

We had white walls in the kitchen, and Charles painted a chef by the gas cooker. The thing we were most pleased about was the dresser; there were drawers for our clothes and shelves for the china. We had a proper tea-set from Waring and Gillow, and a lot of blue plates from Woolworths; our cooking things came from there, too. I had hoped they would give us a set of real silver teaspoons when we bought the wedding-ring, but the jeweller we went to wouldn't, so our spoons came from Woolworths, too.

2

Every evening there was Charles waiting outside the studio where I worked. I could see him from my window, always standing with his back to the railings, looking at the trees in the square garden. The evening before we were married he was there as usual, and as soon as I came out he drew some telegrams out of his pockets and handed them to me. I thought someone must have discovered about our marriage and they were congratulations, but when I read them I felt as frit as Charles looked. One was from my brother saying, 'Do nothing until you hear from me.' I did not worry about this much. As a matter of fact, it was over a month until I did hear from him again, but the other two telegrams were for Charles, one from his father and the other from his mother. They were very angry ones.

Charles had an aunt living quite near, so we decided the best thing would be to go to her flat and ask her advice. It was Emma that I mentioned in the last chapter, and she was the only relation of Charles that liked me. We both admired her immensely. She was a very tall woman with red hair and she wore a cloak and three-cornered hat. She wrote, and was altogether very intellectual and interested in women's rights, but she disliked children, babies in particular, but perhaps that was because she had never had any and couldn't very well now Simeon, her husband, had run away. People always talked about her tragic marriage in hushed voices when she left the room; you were never allowed to mention the name Simeon in front of her. I thought it a wonderful thing that she approved of me and tried not to talk too much in case she discovered how stupid and ignorant I was. She even liked my newts, and sometimes when we went to dinner there I took Great Warty in my pocket; he didn't mind being carried about, and while I had dinner I gave him a swim in the water jug. On this visit I had no newts in my pocket and had the feeling I was going to be most unpopular, but when we arrived at the flat and Charles told her all about the plans for our secret marriage that had somehow gone astray, she was most sympathetic and helpful. We talked for some time. Then she had the bright idea of putting a trunk call through to Charles's father. Charles did this, and said his father didn't sound too dreadful on the 'phone, but had arranged to come to London by train, an early one, and we were to meet him at the station, but we were to do nothing until he came; this didn't sound too frightful to me, although Charles was still very worried. I had a feeling the father would agree to our marriage eventually, partly because Charles's mother disliked me so much. They did not live together, Charles's parents, they simply hated each other; there seemed to be a lot of unhappy marriages in that family, perhaps it was kind of catching.

After we had discussed the trunk call in great detail, Emma said she would meet us at the station to-morrow, and put in a good word for us with Charles's father. I can't go on calling him

Charles's father all the time, so had better call him by his Christian name, which was Paul. He rather resembled Guy Fawkes, and was handsome; women were always falling in love with him and it made Charles's mother even more mad. Her name was Eva. She was like a hard, shiny, rather pretty but horrid beetle, a spoilt, nagging kind of beetle.

We were feeling awfully tired when we left Emma's flat and hardly spoke on the bus going home. Charles came with me to the house where I lived, but I asked him to leave me, as I had so much packing to do, but before he left my landlady came running up the basement stairs; she appeared to be in a great flurry, and said that Charles's mother had been, with a whole host of uncles and aunts, but they had left now and had gone to the house where Charles lived. This was so dreadful, I felt if only we could wait until the morning, but Eva was the kind of woman who would never wait till the morning. My landlady was a kind woman. She did things to people's feet to make them better, and had a room with plaster feet all over the walls. She was most distressed about the invasion of Charles's relations. As a matter of fact, it was she who unintentionally gave us away. That morning Charles's mother had called at his bed-sitting-room, but as he was not there his landlady had sent her on to my house, which was quite near. When my landlady answered the door and Eva explained who she was, she was welcomed in and asked if she had come up for the wedding, so after that Eva spent the rest of the day 'phoning and sending telegrams to everyone she could think of, really rather enjoying herself, I should think; she loved confusion.

While we were discussing this in the hall, there was a great thumping at the door and when it was opened in tumbled all

Charles's maternal relations. I tried to run up the stairs, but they just fell on me like a swarm of angry hornets. One woman in a stiff black hat gripped me by the arm, and I was pushed into the room full of plaster feet. She said I was an uncontrolled little beast, and when was I expecting the baby. Eva said I was not capable of love, only lust, and it was all a trap to catch Charles. I told them I wasn't expecting any babies, but it took a long time to convince them, and they seemed almost disappointed when I did. All the time they tried to make out that I was wicked and sordid to want to marry Charles, and eventually I began to feel I was and my teeth started to chatter. Charles just looked very white and scared; he wasn't very much help. His mother went on talking so much her voice went almost away and she kind of croaked.

When it was about one o'clock my landlady came up and told them they must go away because everyone in the house was complaining about the noise they were making. Eva tried to make me promise I would not see Charles for a year, but all I would say was that I would do whatever Paul said we were to do when he came in the morning. This made her even more angry. She said if he allowed us to marry she would go to the church and stop the marriage. Then they all went, taking Charles with them. I never expected to see him again. I couldn't help wondering what would happen to all our beautiful furniture.

3

Then the morning came and it was light. There were half-packed suitcases all around my bed. The posters that had disguised the ugly wallpaper were lying about in long white scrolls. Great Warty looked at me from his glass house, so I took him out and let him walk up my arm until he fell in the bed, then I made tunnels out of the bedclothes for him to walk slowly through and he looked extra prehistoric. All this time I tried to close my mind that this should have been my wedding morning, also I had to give up my room at twelve o'clock because it had been let to another girl. Actually, I supposed I could live in the flat, but felt this would be impossible without Charles. I never wanted to see it again, also the rent would be far too much for me on my own. I earned two pounds a week and my present room was only fifteen shillings.

Eventually I had a bath and dressed, then I wondered what I should do next, 'phone Mrs Amber, the spiritualist friend, and tell her not to bother about the little reception she had planned to give us after the wedding. Then I started thinking about Charles. Had his mother spirited him away to Wiltshire, and was he as miserable as I was? I heard the front door slam, then there were hurried steps up the stairs and Charles opened the door of my room. At first I thought it was too good to be true and I was imagining things, but it really was Charles. He kissed me and said it was time to meet his father and he thought we should both go to the station. I was so happy to see him again after all my sad thoughts. There he was looking just as if he were going to be married after all. He was wearing his new suit; it had little checks on it and was one of his twenty-first birthday presents, so I pulled off my old yellow linen frock and put on rather a frightful green suit that had a wrap-over skirt that was always coming unwrapped at the wrong moments, but it was my best. Then we hurried away to Paddington Station.

When we arrived there we saw the tall figure of Emma walking up and down the platform, so we went to her and told her all about the dreadful reception we had had after we left her the previous evening. Then the train came in and there was Paul. He was wearing rather an old-fashioned bowler hat, a thing I'd never seen him in before, so I said to Charles, 'That must mean there is going to be a wedding, your father wearing a hat like that.' But when he turned round to talk to Emma, I saw his suit was very shabby; it had been let out at the back with new material and it made a stripe all down his back, so my heart sank, but Charles seemed quite cheerful and said, 'Don't worry. Whatever he says, no one can stop us getting married to-day.'

Paul had a lot of things in the guard's van, a round table and some hampers and some things he was bringing up for a friend; he disposed of these in the cloak-room, then we all went to Hyde Park, or maybe it was some other London park. There we sat on benches and discussed how impossible it was for Charles and me to marry. He gave us quite a long lecture which he enjoyed very much. We didn't listen, but managed to say Yes when it was needed. Charles said, 'Oh yes. Yes indeed,' and the lecture went off very well. He asked us what Eva thought about it all, and he laughed when we told him, and said it was just like Eva. Both he and Emma were rather shocked about the woman in the stiff black hat thinking I was going to have some babies already. After all this talk he said we had better have some lunch, so we went to an Italian café near the Cobden statue. I always thought that statue was of Crippen to point out what a wicked place Camden Town is, but I was quite wrong; Cobden was an eminent Victorian.

I thought it a hopeful sign we were having lunch so near the church we had arranged to be married in, and after we had drunk some wine Paul said: 'Now, Charles, if I allow you two children to marry, I shall stop your allowance. I have enough expense with keeping two homes going as it is, and I can't manage three. If you can't keep yourself now you have come of age and are intending to become a married man, you never will.' Charles said 'Yes, yes' several times – he always did this when he was embarrassed. The thought of saving Charles's allowance seemed to please Paul quite a lot, but we were all in a pretty good mood; we had drunk rather a lot of wine that tasted of ink and the lunch had been quite good; it was an Italian restaurant, not at all the kind of place Paul usually went to. When we were halfway through our coffee he said we had better hurry or we would be too late for the wedding. By this time I had made up my mind he was going to consent to our marriage, and after the remark about Charles's allowance I was quite sure about it.

We left the restaurant in a great hurry, because it was

already half-past two and in England you can't get married after three – something to do with the licensing laws, I should think. The church was next door to my house, so I ran in and perched a beret on my head, because there is another law about that; I put Great Warty in my pocket as a kind of page and ran out of the house. Paul and Charles were waiting outside the church. Paul said he would give me away. We had arranged for rather a handsome actor we knew to do this, but as he seemed to be enjoying himself so much we let him do the giving away and an artist friend of Charles, called James, was the best man.

When we got in the church the priest took Charles right away. I thought it was a trick of his mother's at first, but no one seemed surprised. Then I saw him standing with James very stiff and still. They made me sit in a pew with Paul and I felt a bit scared in case they married me to him by mistake. There were masses of people in the church, most of them uninvited. There was the man who owned the studio where I worked, and some women I sometimes did typing for, also the place was quite stiff with old landladies; some had big hats all covered in feathers. Charles owed rent to quite a lot of them. There was Emma and some of her friends, and my sister Ann. I had asked her to come as a witness. She looked very surprised to see Paul and all those people at a secret wedding. I smiled at her to show it was all right. I could see Mrs Amber sitting by herself with a worried look on her face; I could guess she was worried about all the people in the church, in case they all came to the reception; she was only expecting about seven.

Then I forgot all about the people in the church because lovely little noises came, kind of singing, chirping noises. I saw all up in the roof there were masses of little birds, all singing and chirping in the most delightful manner. I felt so glad we hadn't paid extra for the beastly organ and hoped so much we would make a success of our marriage after the birds being so nice about it.

A little man called a verger came and told us the time had come to go up the aisle. I looked round the church quickly to make sure Eva wasn't around somewhere. She had said she would say she knew a just cause and impediment why we should not marry and I was dreading a scene like there is in *Jane Eyre*, but she did not appear to be anywhere unless she was hiding. I soon found myself going up the aisle very fast on Paul's arm. I hoped my boss couldn't see the seam down Paul's back. People kept smiling at me and I wasn't sure if you had to acknowledge them or not; the landlady before the last shouted out, 'Would you like a kitten born on your wedding day?' as I passed, so I shouted back, 'Yes,' just as I reached the altar. Charles was still there and the priest and James, who produced the wedding-ring. Charles and I had to do a lot of talking, but it was not difficult, because we said it after the priest, and we were married in no time, quite safely, because Eva was not there to say about just causes and impediments.

When we got to the vestry Paul kissed me and I felt rather sad because it should have been Charles, but he was looking rather white and dazed, also he hadn't enough money to pay them for marrying us. It was quite a lot of money they wanted – about seventeen-and-six, I believe, but we borrowed it from James. Of course, we need not have paid, because they couldn't unmarry us if we hadn't. I expect people do that sometimes, but it would be rather unpleasant.

As soon as the wedding was over we all went to Mrs Amber's flat in Buckingham Gate. We went in taxis, buses and Emma's car. Although the flat was very small the reception was quite a success and Mrs Amber did not seem to mind that the party had grown so large; she got on rather well with Paul. I was so thrilled by my wedding-ring I didn't notice the guests much. I found a quiet corner where I could look at my left hand in all sorts of positions. The effect was rather spoilt because there was a lot of sea-green paint under my nails that I had not had time to get out.

After a time Paul said he would like to see the flat, so we said Goodbye to the guests and took a taxi to the station to collect the things for his friend, but when we arrived at Haverstock Hill it turned out they were meant for us, so he must have made up his mind about us before he left home. There was a dear little oak tip-up table, and we were so pleased with it. In the hamper was linen and some glass and china, also there was an enormous bunch of asparagus.

He thought our flat most attractive, and before he left it was arranged that we should spend the next weekend at his house in the Cotswolds, so it was good to think that we were not at all in disgrace with him. After he left we walked round the shops and did our first shopping. There was a street of small shops quite near, one or two of each kind, even a draper's and cobbler's. I still had my two pounds wages in my bag, so we could buy quite a lot. I didn't know much about meat, so when we got to the butcher's, I said, 'Can I have a small joint of bones stuck together?' and the butcher told me that kind of meat is called best end of neck of lamb.

In the evening Ann came and helped us unpack and arrange

14

things, and to talk about the wedding. We ate heaps of asparagus and drank Chianti which came out of a nice bottle dressed
in straw; we kept that bottle for years. We were awfully tired and
went to bed as soon as she left, but the divan we had bought on
hire purchase was not comfortable at all, because we had no
mattress on top and the clothes kept slipping off, also the sheets
were new and stiff and smelt funny. We were much too tired to
make love and it was not at all the kind of wedding night I had
read about, but eventually we bought a mattress and were able
to tuck the clothes in and the sheets were washed and didn't
smell and we became proper married people.

4

Sophia Fairclough was my new name and quite soon I became used to it and to being called 'Mrs' and wearing a wedding-ring. Already, after a few weeks' married life, my saucepans had burnt marks on them. I had hoped to keep them always shiny, because I had a stupid feeling that as long as I could keep them like new my marriage would stay the same, but in spite of the saucepans we were quite happy. Sometimes I worried about money a little because my weekly two pounds did not go very far, but we had some cheques in one of the dresser drawers, and whenever we ran out of money we asked my sister Ann to cash one. She earned enough to have a banking account and was a real bachelor girl with a flat. She was two years older than I and rather efficient at her job on a woman's weekly. She collected material for a page 'Ways of wasting not more than five shillings' and all the articles on the page had captions underneath like this: 'This dainty little butter-dish made of leather costs but 2/11' or 'Wouldn't the kiddies just love this jolly little squeaking mouse – a bargain at 4/9'. They gave her the things she wrote about quite often, so her flat was full of gadgets, and she had a box under her bed simply stiff with things to give people for Christmas. Before our marriage Charles used to paint and draw me quite a lot, but now we were living together I had to pose in every imaginable position. In the middle of washing the supper things, Charles would say 'Don't move', and I would have to keep quite still, with my hands in the water, until he finished drawing me, or I might be preparing the supper and everything would get all held up. He painted me in the bath once and I have never been so clean before or since. Sometimes when I woke in the morning, there would be Charles painting me asleep. That was the most comfortable way to be painted, but it made me late for work. When I was out during the day he liked to paint still lives. He would arrange a group on a cushion – a melon, a banana and some carrots and perhaps a kipper or an egg, but the kitten, Matthew, would eat the fish in the night and play football with the fruit and Charles would be most upset, although he was rather batty about the kitten usually; he was called Matthew after the church we were married in, he was grey and dainty. Most mornings Charles would walk with me to Chalk Farm station and Matthew would follow about halfway and wait for Charles until he returned, and they would be company for each other during the day. Charles stayed at home painting most of the day; he did the shopping, too. Sometimes he went to commercial studios in search of work, but nothing ever came of it; not that he really expected anything, this was the time of the Great Depression or Slump, but there were still a few cheques in the drawer.

On Saturday afternoon I had a holiday and we would give the flat a great clean and shop, and on Sunday we went for long walks on the Heath or read and were lazy by the gas fire. In the evening Ann or other friends came to supper.

At first everything I cooked tasted very strongly of soap, I can't think why, but soon I became quite a good cook. During the week I was so hungry when I returned home I couldn't attempt anything that took a long time, but I used to experiment in the weekend. Quite often James came to dinner and we would discuss cooking. He was a very good cook and could even make bread. One evening I returned to find the windows streaming with steam and the most awful smell of burnt frying. Even the cat had run away. I walked through a haze to the kitchen to find Charles trying to curry eggs from Mrs Beeton's cookery book. He had been at it since four o'clock and he was just burning his third lot of eggs, but we ate them.

It was a long time before the smell of burnt curry left the flat.

One Saturday, after we had been married about two months, we thought we would skip the housework, so Charles met me and we had lunch in Charlotte Street and then went to the Tate. We returned home with masses of postcards in time for tea. I glanced through the windows of the flat as we passed on our way to the side door. To my surprise the room was full of people. Charles said, 'It must be Mummy, I can hear her voice.' He was quite right. There was Eva surrounded by the same relations she had brought with her the night before the wedding. My first thought was, 'Well, they can't unmarry us now.' Then I remembered the flat was all dusty and uncleaned. My heart sank right down to my rather holey shoes. If only I had known they were coming and had polished the floor and had everything grand and tidy. I had thought it too good to be true that Eva had ignored us all this time, although I believe she sometimes wrote pained letters to Charles.

Charles went in first and I followed feeling pretty scared. Eva kissed Charles and then me, so I knew it was meant to be a friendly visit. I couldn't help feeling glad I'd smudged her lipstick when she kissed me, I knew she would feel pretty mad when she arrived home and saw her face. I started muttering about the place being untidy and that I would have made a cake if I'd known they were coming, but she said it did not matter as she had imagined it much worse, but she had had to hunt everywhere for the teaspoons. I could imagine her going through the dresser drawers, looking at all my shabby clothes and holding them up for her relations to see.

She said she admired the flat very much, but thought the hard chairs rather uncomfortable and she couldn't understand how we could sleep on such a small divan and why didn't we have a charwoman. Then Edmund, the husband of Stiff-black-hat, said he was sure Eva would be able to give me some useful hints on economical housekeeping. As Eva was quite famous for her extravagance in dress and home, I was rather interested to hear what she would have to say. She cleared her throat once or twice, and said something about poor people should eat a lot of herrings, as they were most nutritious, also she had heard poor people ate heaps of sheep's heads and she went on to ask if I ever cooked them. I said I would rather be dead than cook or eat a sheep's head; I'd seen them in butchers' shops with awful eyes and bits of wool sticking to their skulls. After that helpful hints for the poor were forgotten, because Charles told her about our visit to Paul. She was most interested, because she wanted to know how he was situated for money, because she needed her allowance increasing. Charles and I both assured her he was living in the most abject poverty and his house was understaffed and his car just falling to bits, so she began to worry in case her allowance was cut.

Then Edmund started asking Charles about his prospects. Had he a job in view? Had he sold any paintings? Had he any prospects at all? So Charles had to pretend things were much better than they were, and he talked very brightly and rather unconvincingly about his future. As a matter of fact Edmund had business troubles of his own; I couldn't help wishing Charles would ask him a few questions about his financial position.

At last Stiff-black-hat, who had not spoken all this time, said it was time to go and dress for dinner. Eva was staying with them for the night. All this time she had been sitting on the unpaid-for divan, looking around with cold blue eyes, her thin white lips tightly pressed together. I had no relations with the exception of a sister and brother. They had all died for one reason or another, but I felt Charles had enough for us both.

There was a great searching about the room for Eva's belongings. Then the kitten was found asleep on her coat and there had to be a great brushing to get the hairs off, but at last they left and it felt as if there had been a great wind which had suddenly ceased.

After this first visit Eva and I had a kind of truce; she continued to criticise and talk at me, but as she did the same to everyone she knew, even Charles, I couldn't object too much. Although most of Charles's relations came from Wiltshire they used to come to London very frequently. They all talked and asked questions about our financial position and took the line of 'I hope you are looking after dear Charles properly', or 'What a lucky girl you are to have married into our family.' In those days I was too timid to say much, but I used to resent it all the more and sometimes, after they left, I would be nervy and resentful with Charles. Also they would keep suggesting impractical ways we could earn extra money. They sent cuttings from the *Daily Mail* about how I could make sweets or gloves at home and make a fortune, or complicated rackets for Charles to sell note-cases to our friends on commission. As none of our friends had any notes, he wouldn't have done very well from it.

Except when his relations came fussing around Charles was quite happy just painting away, and as long as I earned two pounds a week and there were a few cheques in the drawer he hadn't a care in the world. He was very loving and gentle with me. One day we went to the sea for the day with James and a huge wave knocked me down when we were bathing. He was dreadfully distressed and kept asking if I was all right. I liked him to be concerned for me, because it was a very long time since anyone had been. I'd been living alone in bed-sitting-rooms since I was seventeen and it had been rather a hard life and lonely sometimes, too.

5

After about ten weeks of married life I began to feel rather sick, not of Charles or married life – just sick in myself. At first it was just a whisper of sickness and I began to think I was imagining it, then I thought maybe it was strawberries; they were very cheap that year, there must have been what they call in the newspapers a 'glut', we even ate strawberries for breakfast. One Sunday morning the milkman left a pint of cream instead of milk; it was marvellous. We ate everything simply smothered in cream; the kitten had a share, too, but the next day I felt even more sick. Then the whisper became very loud and I became really sick. It was so difficult at work, because I had to keep running to the lavatory. I felt a little better in the evening, but so tired, all I wanted to do was to go to bed. There were big black rings round my eyes.

· The girls I worked with said I should see a doctor; most likely he would have a nice surprise for me. One morning I fainted when I got out of bed. Charles was very scared and said I was to stay in bed. I didn't like to stay away from the studio in case they found how well they could get on without me and gave me the

22

sack. I hadn't been working very well lately, but it just seemed like heaven to stay in bed, so I did.

Charles said he would fetch a doctor. We had noticed a brass plate a little further up the road. Quite soon he returned with a proper doctor, complete with a black bag, a morning coat and pin-striped trousers, but he had a sad face. He talked to us for a little time to put us at our ease, then he sent Charles out while he examined me and asked a few questions. When Charles returned he had a very stiff bunch of maidenhair fern and carnations in his hand. The doctor had reserved his verdict until his return. Then he told us we were going to have a baby; it was going to come in about seven months. Charles's white pointed face went even more so and I felt frightened, trapped and excited all at once.

The doctor gave a few hints and words of advice, and said I was to visit him in about a month. Then he had gone and we were left alone, but we were not alone any more. Charles said, 'Oh dear, what will the family say? How I dislike the idea of being a Daddy and pushing a pram!' So I said, 'I don't want to be a beastly Mummy either; I shall run away.' Then I remembered if I ran away the baby would come with me wherever I went. It was a most suffocating feeling and I started to cry.

Charles kissed me then and said it was no use crying about something that was not going to happen for seven months, I might have a miscarriage before then. I was almost more scared of having a miscarriage than having a baby, so I went on crying.

The next day I went back to work and told the girls what the doctor said had happened to me. They laughed and said they knew that already. They teased me about the baby rather a lot, but were kind really. If only they hadn't told me such dreadful stories about childbirth. Frightful things seemed to have happened to their mothers and friends. They made it seem almost impossible to have a baby that was not dead or deformed in some way. I began to think mine would at least have a hare-lip. I kept seeing people in the street with them, and everywhere I looked there were hunchbacks and cripples. There were lots of daddy-long-legs about that year, and they kept coming in the flat, from Primrose Hill, I expect. I got an idea that if one touched me the baby would be marked in that place, or if one touched my mouth it would have a hare-lip. I screamed every time I saw one, and I kept jumping up in the night and putting the light on to make sure none had got in the room. I had to sleep with my head under the bedclothes in case one touched my lips when I was asleep. Charles got very angry with me and said I was stupid and hysterical, as no doubt I was. Most fortunately, Matthew – the kitten – began to take a great interest in daddy-long-legs and used to catch them in his mouth and dash about with all the legs sticking out like a moustache. As he chewed, the legs gradually disappeared. He pounced on each one as soon as it appeared in the flat. I was so grateful to him and let him sleep on the bed as a reward for his service.

Poor little Matthew! One morning he came part of the way down the hill with me, as usual, and never returned. Charles spent all the day searching for him, and the next morning someone came to say he had been run over. Charles was even more sad than I about this misfortune. We bought a catfish and called it Greedy Min and put it on the mantelpiece by Great Warty, but it wasn't much of a companion to Charles in the daytime.

One night, a few weeks later, we awoke to find a large ginger cat asleep on the divan, so we let him stay and in the morning he was still there. We called him Ambassador. At first he seemed very old and feeble. He had bald patches and scabs, and sat by the gas fire all day with his head hanging low. His teeth fell out one by one. They used to sound like little bullets as they fell in the dustpan when I swept the carpet. Quite soon he started to change rapidly – beautiful new teeth came and his fur grew dense and his tail all bushy. Then his thin old face became completely round, and he was a cat to be proud of. One disadvantage about him was, he used to bring all his dirty old friends in as soon as our backs were turned, and they smelt rather. Still, we were glad to have a cat again, even one with smelly friends.

6

After about three months I forgot about feeling sick, but the baby weighed on my mind quite a lot. Before I married Charles I used to hope I would have masses of children. I thought it would be nice always to have at least one baby and quite a number of older children all developing in their individual ways, but before we were married Charles told me he never wanted to have any children, and I saw they would not fit in with the kind of life we would lead, so I just hoped none would come to such unsuitable parents – anyway, not for years. I had a kind of idea if you controlled your mind and said 'I won't have any babies' very hard, they most likely wouldn't come. I thought that was what was meant by birth-control, but by this time I knew that idea was quite wrong.

Sometimes I would find myself quite looking forward to the baby, and long to see and hold it in my arms, but when I told Charles I felt like this, he was annoyed and made me feel I had betrayed him in some way and had got all sentimental.

So far even Charles's mother had not noticed anything wrong with me, and I knew if it escaped her black, sharp eyes I was safe from the rest of his family for some time to come. It was a whole month since I had seen the doctor, so one evening on my way home I called at his house. He had no waiting-room, so I sat in the drawing-room by the fire and talked to his comfortable wife. When the doctor came in he was very pleasant and said he would get me into one of the big hospitals to have the baby and it would cost hardly anything at all. We talked quite a lot, and I told them how my cooking used to taste of soap, but was improving now. The doctor said next time I came he would show me how to cook real Indian curry; he had learnt how to make it when he lived there, so I thought, 'That is why he looks so yellow and sad.' I had noticed people who have lived in hot countries for some time often look like that; perhaps it does something to their livers.

But I never learnt how to make that curry, because the doctor and his wife both committed suicide. The man did it first, by doing something to his arm with a needle, and when his poor wife found him all dead like that, she gassed herself. We felt dreadfully shocked and sad about this and I felt more worried about the baby than ever.

Then the autumn came and the cheques in the dresser drawer were all gone. There was only a little box with some Spade guineas in it; that's all that was left. They had been a wedding present and we had hoped we would never have to spend them. Charles was very bright and kept saying something would turn up. He did get a job in a commercial studio, but it only lasted a week. He had to draw brushes – scrubbing ones – all day, and he wasn't very suitable for drawing brushes, so that wasn't any good. Then he got two hanging signs for tearooms to paint and earned ten pounds, so we became full of hope again and had supper at Bertorelli's, and drank sour Barbera to celebrate. I bought some tiny pearl buttons and some fine lace trimming for the baby. It was at about this time that it started moving about inside me and it felt strange and rather delightful. I began to wonder what kind it would be. I knew Charles never liked me to mention it, but it was rather difficult to forget it when it was moving about like that, so I did ask which kind he wanted. He said he wouldn't mind so much if it was a girl and had long hair. After that I hoped very much it would be a long-haired girl. I decided to call her Willow, which I thought a graceful, romantic kind of name.

So far we had only taken my sister Ann and James into our confidence about the baby, but I felt the time had almost come when Charles's family would notice I was getting full of babies, and they wouldn't be quite so upset about it if we had made a few arrangements about a hospital and pram and things like that, so thought it would be a good idea to ask some of our friends' advice about these things. Most of our friends were bachelor artists, with the exception of Mrs Amber, and I knew she would suggest me having the baby in some remote Italian village on the top of a mountain or else in a magic stream with silver leaves in my hair. Charles said the most sensible person to ask was Francis. He was a young portrait painter who had had more experience than we had and liked to give us advice on all kinds of subjects, and it was usually quite good advice.

Francis was rather overwhelmed when Charles told him we were expecting a baby, but you could see he was flattered we had asked his advice. He said he would let us know in a few days the best and cheapest way to have babies, and he thought he knew someone who would give us a pram their child had outgrown.

Two days later he came to see us and brought his sister with him. She was a large, handsome, efficient kind of girl of about thirty. They had been asking all their friends about having babies and had discovered an old woman of eighty, who was very rich and ugly and kind and abrupt all at the same time. She spent her days fixing up young Jewish mothers in hospitals and doing other good deeds, too, but the maternity part was her most important work. Francis's sister had spoken to her about me and she had agreed to help, even if I wasn't a Jewess. Quite soon I went to see her and found she was a little old hunched-back woman with a huge nose and twisted hands. Her house was large, dark and breathless and the furniture massive and sad. There were bead curtains, stuffed birds, ferns and Indian brass objects all creeping about the place, but the old woman was full of vitality. She was like a dark gleaming jewel in a dusty old velvet case. Within a few minutes she had given me a letter to a Dr Wombat of King Edward's Hospital, and had promised me a cot and some baby clothes and said it was a pity I was not a Jewess and hustled me out.

I arranged to have a morning off from the studio. Also I told my boss I was expecting a baby, and he said I had better leave at Christmas. I did not like to tell him how much we depended on the money I was earning or he might have thought Charles wasn't a good artist, but it was rather a blow to know I was leaving at Christmas. I had hoped they would let me stay till the baby came and perhaps let me come back after and leave it in a pram by the railings while I was working.

I was very frightened when the morning came that I was to visit the hospital, and I walked past several times before I dared go in. It was an enormous red brick building and I kind of felt they would never let me out again when I walked in through the large front door, but I was out very soon because a porter said, 'You can't come in here; you must go to the side entrance in the basement.' So I went down some depressing steps and through a door with OUT PATIENTS on it. I showed an official-looking woman my note and she told me to sit on a bench with a lot of other women who were new patients.

We had to wait a very long time, so they all started talking to each other. I didn't like to talk because I felt I was a fraud. They were all so bulging with baby and I hardly showed at all. Quite a number of them had had children before, and they all seemed to have been in and out of hospital all their lives. They talked very knowingly about how they had routed matrons and sisters, and how they had told the doctors what they thought of them. They were full of complaints about hospital treatment and food, but in spite of all this talk I had the feeling they really rather liked hospitals and were glad to be back again.

It was very depressing and dreary sitting in that passage. One of the women fainted. I noticed some of them were carrying glasses of what I thought was lemonade, so I asked where I could go to get some, but they all shrieked with laughter at me, so I didn't dare to speak again.

After a very long time the official woman came and said we were to go into cubicles and undress. We were allowed to keep our vests on. I went into one of the cubicles which was like a wooden bathing hut. There were three other women there. They all wore big grey corsets, so it took them ages to undress. Some of them rubbed their legs to get the red mark of their garters off. They said the doctors were cross with you if you wore garters. I can't think why they did wear them, because they had forests of suspenders hanging from the grey corsets. I had no stockings and hardly any underclothes, so it did not take me long to undress and put on one of the pink-cotton dressing gowns that were hanging up for our use – they were very short but clean.

When I returned to the passage I was given a glass and told to put a specimen in it. I realised what a fool I had made of myself about the lemonade – if I had been dressed I would have left the hospital. After about another hour I did get examined by Dr Wombat. He was young and charming and cheered me up quite a lot. I was fortunate and managed to escape being examined by the students, but on later visits I had quite a lot of this. I noticed the women students were not so gentle as the men and usually hurt rather, but perhaps this is not general. I may have been unlucky in the women students that came my way.

When I left the hospital they gave me a card which was pink and had my name on it. This card had to be produced when I returned to the hospital in labour. It said I would not be admitted without it. I felt sure I would lose it in all the hurry and pain and I would be turned away at the door. They gave me a pamphlet, too. It said I must always clean my teeth, with salt if I couldn't afford tooth-paste, and I mustn't take dangerous drugs to try to produce a miscarriage. There was some other advice about if you started to bleed, I think.

31

7

A few weeks before Christmas there was a great stir in Charles's family. Stiff-black-hat died. She caught 'flu, and it made her dead in three days, although she was only forty-four and not due to die for years. As soon as Eva heard the news she came to London to stay with her brother Edmund. She 'phoned and asked us to come and console him, too. I didn't much like going to a house with dead people in it, but Charles said we had better go, all the same.

When we arrived at the gloomy Kensington house, they were all having tea – Edmund, Eva and Stiff-black-hat's mother, who lived with them. Edmund looked very tired, but Eva was full of vitality, and was telling him just what to do about the funeral, and advising him to sell the house and sack the servants, sell the furniture, get a housekeeper and give away the dog. He seemed rather dazed, and beyond saying Yes occasionally, took very little notice. I wondered what Eva's ideas about the old mother were. You could hardly sell or give her away. She didn't seem at all put out by her daughter's death, and kept on stuffing away at little pink cakes. When she had quite finished eating she started chuckling to herself, and said, 'Who would have thought it? Who would have thought I would have outlived my youngest daughter? I shall go and live at the Regent Palace Hotel and have a gay time.'

I felt now that Eva was so interested in the funeral and Edmund's affairs, it would be a good moment to tell her about the coming baby. I waited until she should cease talking for a moment. I had to wait rather a long time, but eventually she did and I found myself almost shouting, 'I am going to have a baby in fourteen weeks.' My news caused a great commotion and for the time being Eva quite forgot about death and funerals, and she left Edmund in peace and he fell asleep with his head hanging over the teacups.

Eva was rather impressed that we had made all the necessary arrangements. I did not tell her that I would shortly be leaving my job, because already she had said that penniless people had no right to have children. She didn't seem to think it was Charles's baby – only mine, because later on, when I was upstairs putting on my coat, she kissed me quite kindly, but spoilt it by saying, 'I shall never forgive you, Sophia, for making my son a father at twenty-one.' I almost added, 'And you a grandmother at forty-six.'

Charles went to the funeral. He had to hire the grim clothes, but I didn't see him in them, because I was at work. He told me all about it when I returned home in the evening. He said Eva had told all her relations about the coming baby, and they had asked him masses of questions about how he was going to support a wife and family. They had given him some money, though, four pounds in all. I was glad to hear this, as we had only one golden guinea left in the dresser drawer, but my gladness did not last long, because it turned out he had already spent the money on some paints, brushes, books and an enormous walnut cake from Fullers.

We had the walnut cake and coffee for supper and while we ate he told me that Stiff-black-hat had left the house and furniture to a woman friend. Apparently Edmund had turned this property over to her, so now he had nothing. Charles said he did not seem to mind very much. It was a most gloomy, depressing house, stiff with heavy dark furniture. There were sideboards with prancing bronze horses on them and silver-plated biscuit barrels; the mantelpieces were made of black and green marble, and the curtains were of black or maroon plush, so really it was a jolly good thing he had lost the house.

He also told me that the old mother-in-law had had her hair dyed black and really had gone to have her 'gay time' at the Regent Palace Hotel.

We sat talking over the walnut cake for some time, and Charles said that now his mother knew about the baby the time had come to tell the rest of his family, so I fetched some ink and paper and we started writing letters all among the walnut cake and coffee cups. I didn't like it to seem as if I hadn't any relations to write to, so I wrote to my brother. I did not expect an answer, and was surprised when I received a letter from his wife a few days later. She wrote suggesting I paid them a visit after the baby's arrival. I was rather pleased about this. They had a nice country house. I had never been there, but had heard about it from Ann, who stayed there quite often. I think the reason they had not asked me before was that they thought I was a bit 'arty' and odd, but expect they hoped now I was becoming a mother I would improve.

34

The person we were most frit of telling about the baby was Charles's Aunt Emma; she so disliked babies, and we knew we would go down deeply in her estimation when she knew we were having one. We had been to her flat quite a lot since we were married, and she had sometimes taken us to the Arts Theatre on Sunday evenings. Just lately I felt I was enjoying this hospitality under false pretences. Charles undertook to call round one afternoon at tea-time and tell her the dreadful truth. I thought this immensely brave of him. She received the news very coldly, and made it quite plain she was most disappointed in us. We saw her very seldom after this.

8

Paul was a bit het up when he heard we were going to have a family, but at the same time, you could tell from reading his letter he was rather amused at the idea of being a grandfather, as long as it didn't cost him anything. Ann had known she was going to be an aunt for some time, and she kept showering me with motherly magazines published by the firm she worked for. They – the magazines, not the firm – were very sentimental, and called babies 'little treasures', and the walking ones were 'toddlers'. There were pages about the glories of motherhood. Also there were letters from mothers asking advice – 'Was it true that if you eat apples before your baby was born, you would have a dwarf?' Or 'Why does my baby cry after eating sardines?' There were stories, too, telling how much more men loved their wives if they were domesticated and had some children. In some of the stories the wives used to prefer going to work every day instead of doing the housework and having a baby. Their husbands always left these selfish wives, but just at the last minute before anything drastic happened, the wife would become all domesticated or find she was having a 'little treasure' and the husband

36

would come back. All these stories had happy endings, which was a good thing.

By now it was nearly Christmas and the lease of our flat ended at that date. We felt it was not worth renewing, because it would be too small for three people. Charles hated the idea of moving and suggested we kept the baby in the cupboard, but after reading all those magazines I knew it wasn't a good idea, and made the reluctant Charles go flat-hunting. I couldn't go myself because of work. Quite soon he reported he had found a super studio flat that had belonged to a well-known poster artist. I thought it sounded very expensive, but he said it was only twenty-five shillings a week, so on Saturday we both went to see it. It was at the top of a large red brick house off Finchley Road. There was a huge studio, bedroom and kitchen and bathroom, and cupboard for unsightly brooms, as the landlady pointed out. I was most impressed, so we told the landlady we would have it, but when we were discussing the rent we discovered it was £96 a year. Charles said he thought that worked out at twenty-five shillings a week, and the landlady said, 'I should think not, indeed!' and hustled us downstairs.

Poor Charles, he was so disappointed, but eventually he found an attic flat in Fortune Green. It had three rooms and a kitchen on the landing. I had to work overtime the day we moved. It seemed strange to leave home in the morning and return to a new one in the evening. When I arrived James was cooking sausages on the landing by the light of a candle, and Charles had got one room straight and a fire going. We had dis-covered you had to pay a deposit at the electric light place, so we had to do without any till after Christmas, when we hoped we would have some money left over from Christmas presents.

I looked about for the ginger cat, Ambassador, but he was nowhere to be seen. Then Charles told me a sad thing. When he had arrived holding Great Warty under one arm and the cat under the other the landlady had said, 'I never allow pets. Take the creature away at once.' He did get Great Warty in by pretending he was a goldfish, but she insisted on him taking Ambassador away at once, so he left James to do the unpacking and took the poor cat to my old landlady and asked her to find a good home for him, and afterwards we heard he had a very good home by the British Museum. We missed him very much, and I hoped she wouldn't expect me to give the baby away when it came.

It was a difficult journey to the studio from Fortune Green and the flat wasn't so nice as the one on Haverstock Hill. We had to share the bathroom with lots of other people, but the view from the small bedroom window was marvellous. You could see right across London. On fine days we could even see green fields in the distance. We used to spend hours picking out various buildings. The Crystal Palace was the most conspicuous.

Living in such an out-of-the-way place lost us quite a number of our friends, but Ann and the faithful James came quite frequently. James was teaching me how to knit baby clothes, but I didn't get on very well when he wasn't there, but I did manage two vests that resembled badly made porridge.

Francis and his sister came sometimes, too. They came one evening soon after we had moved. They were accompanied by an Austrian woman. She was a portrait painter and always looking for new models, so she asked me if I would sit for her when my job ended. I was delighted. I had been so worried about how we would manage when my salary ended. A model's fee was half-a-crown an hour and she said she would need me quite a lot and would introduce me to other portrait painters when she had finished painting me. I just felt so happy, as if a great weight had gone from my mind; now I could tell Charles's family I was still able to earn money and not be a drag on Charles.

Two days before Christmas I left the studio where I had been working for three years. I told them Charles had plenty of commissions coming in and I was looking forward to a rest. The other unmarried girls were quite envious and said what fun it must be to be married and going to have a baby. I said it was marvellous, and they must all come and see me when it had arrived. I said Goodbye to the boss and he gave me an extra two pounds on my last week's wages and shook hands with me. Then I threw my paint-stained overall in the dustbin and never saw any of them again.

Both Charles's parents wanted us to stay with them for Christmas, so we went to Wiltshire for a week and spent a difficult time dividing ourselves between them; we even had to eat two Christmas dinners. Although both Charles's parents tried to be kind, we did not enjoy the holiday at all. For one reason Paul's wife was a managing, domestic kind of woman. She kept asking how I did my various household tasks and when I told her she would say it was all wrong and show me the proper efficient way. Some of the things she taught me I couldn't remember. She must have shown me how to fold a gentleman's shirt at least a dozen times, but even now I can't fold the wretched things, but I can mend an electric fire or burst pipes (lead ones) and make plaster casts and regulate pianos, and masses more things she can't do, but people are always shocked if you don't do the things they do properly. She was quite a generous woman really,

39

and kept wanting to give me things for the baby, nice things, but Charles said I wasn't to accept them, because Eva would not approve. He had always been brought up to hate his father's second wife, and when we went to see Eva, she would say 'How is that dreadful woman?' and make fun of her. She would ask questions about how the house was furnished, and get in a temper and say 'Do you mean to tell me that creature is using my dressing-table?' or silver, or whatever it was she was enquiring about, although she had nothing to worry about really, because she had had much more than her half of the furniture from the old house she used to live in when she was married to Paul. Another thing that upset her a lot was that since Paul had married a second time he ran a car and a house telephone. Both these things he had refused to have while they were living together. I expect he would have let her have these things if she hadn't nagged so much for them.

When we got back to Paul's house, Mrs Paul would say, 'And how was Her Ladyship? Is it true that she has a new fur coat?' Then she would go on for hours with much bitterness about how much alimony Eva had and how unhappy she made Paul when she was married to him. I couldn't bear all this and said I must return to London because I was due for another examination at the hospital, and Charles said it was most important I didn't miss it, so we went home to have some peace.

9

This book does not seem to be growing very large although I have got to Chapter Nine. I think this is partly because there isn't any conversation. I could just fill pages like this:

'I am sure it is true,' said Phyllida.

'I cannot agree with you,' answered Norman.

'Oh, but I know I am right,' she replied.

'I beg to differ,' said Norman sternly. That is the kind of stuff that appears in real people's books. I know this will never be a real book that business men in trains will read, the kind of business men that wear stiff hats with curly brims and little breathing holes let in the side. I wish I knew more about words. Also I wish so much I had learnt my lessons at school. I never did, and have found this such a disadvantage ever since. All the same, I am going on writing this book even if business men scorn it.

After we had returned from our Christmas visits, the Austrian woman kept her promise and wrote and asked me to sit for my portrait. She painted several pictures of me and I enjoyed spending the day at her studio. There was a large gas-fire burning away in the grate, not one like ours that kept on going out because it wanted more shillings. I enjoyed the warmth so much and there was lunch, too. We used to go to a small restaurant nearby where she used to meet several of her girl friends. I was rather shy for them to see I did not pay for lunch myself, but they did not seem to notice.

When she had finished the third portrait of me she gave me an introduction to an R.A. she knew. I was nervous when I called at his studio. I need not have been; he was most kind and so was his wife. He said he would paint me straight away, and that he would like to paint me with the baby when it arrived. These people gave me lunch, too, and these free meals were a great help, because I had grown dreadfully hungry lately and we were rather short of food at home. All the golden guineas had gone now and we only had the little I earned as a model. With this we had to pay for food, light and heat, and laundry and of course rent. Sometimes we were several weeks behind and the landlady would ask us for money each time we went in or out of the house. I would hear her talking about us to the other people who lived on the floor below and felt dreadfully ashamed. Charles did not mind. He just said she was a silly old bitch. As soon as Charles started to paint he forgot about the cold and money worries. That is how artists should be, but I was only a commercial artist, so I went on worrying. In any case, there was no time for me to paint, because there was all the work of the flat, and shopping and cooking to do when I returned home in the evening.

When things were looking pretty grim, Francis put some hack lettering work in Charles's way, so we were able to pay the rent that was owing. Then another friend wanted their flat redecorating and asked Charles to do it. They paid him ten pounds for this work and it seemed like a fortune to us, and I was able to keep back a little of the money I earned to get a few things for the baby. I already had a cot, given to me by the old woman of eighty with the twisted hands, so I bought some most attractive blue spotted muslin to trim it with, and I bought a nice soft feather pillow for a mattress. I made a little pillow for its head out of three bullrushes' heads I had saved for this purpose, and it was beautiful. Several people had given me baby clothes. Most of them were rather clumsy and coarse, not the kind of things I had seen in the baby-shop windows; although I put new ribbons on them they were still ugly. I had knitted some little jackets and vests, but they didn't look quite right. The nappies were new. Some were just like towels, but the ones Paul's wife had given me were rather grand and called Harrington Squares. Charles said I was not to write and thank her for them, but I did.

I packed a suitcase all ready to take to the hospital in case the baby came too soon. The hospital said I wasn't to take any baby clothes, just some night-dresses and toilet things, and a teapot and bed jacket. I longed for a pretty bed jacket, one all trimmed with fluffy swans-down. One of Charles's aunts sent me rather a horrible kind of roly-poly affair – a kind of shawl with sleeves – made of stiff, scratchy wool, so I had to pack that. I also put two half-crowns in the case to make sure we had enough money for a taxi to take me to the hospital.

By this time I was growing rather large, not only in the tummy, but behind as well. This made me extremely sad when I saw myself in shop windows – luckily we had not got any long mirrors at home. Charles used to call me 'Dumpling', and his mother often said I was a dumpy little person, and if the baby took after me she couldn't possibly be called Willow, which was

43

a ridiculous name in any case. They seemed to forget how slim I used to be. My waist used to be only nineteen inches before I became all stiff with babies. Eva said, 'Why on earth don't you wear a maternity gown? You can't go about like that.' Needless to say, I couldn't afford one. There was one nice thing about being such a funny shape – it made strangers very kind. Busmen were so careful helping me in and out of buses, and policemen held up the traffic when I wanted to cross the road; fortunately, it was just before they had traffic lights. The people who served in shops were most kind, too.

Eva wanted to come and stay a week before the baby was due – to help. This worried me a lot. I knew she was trying to be kind, but already she had stayed in the flat once and it was most difficult. For one thing she would spend hours in the bathroom and when at last she did come out, it would be left in the most dreadful mess, talcum powder spilt over the floor and the bath all scummy. Before I could get down there to clear it up, some of the people we shared the bathroom with would go and complain to the landlady about the state of the bathroom, and there would be a lot of trouble. Another thing – we only had six towels, and as they were all small, she would use the whole lot for her bath. Then they were draped all over the flat to dry. The absence of a long mirror upset her a lot, too, but it wasn't only the absence of a long mirror; there were dozens of things missing in our home – sheets, for instance, we only had about two pairs, and one pair was always in the wash, so when Eva came to stay we gave her the sheets and slept between blankets, and as she expected at least two pillows, we gave her ours.

We did not mind the temporary discomfort, but I did mind dreadfully when she discovered these things. She had always had

44

so much herself, she just couldn't understand how difficult it is to be poor and how the merest necessity becomes a luxury. She thought the lack of essentials in the flat was due to the fact that I was a bad housekeeper and did not know how civilised people lived.

I found it very difficult to tell her that I did not want her to visit us so near the baby's birth, but just had to trust that it would arrive early before she came, and I did all I could to make this come about. I even went to the fair at Hampstead Heath on Easter Saturday. It was a very early Easter that year. Charles went with me, and I had to hold on to his arm to help me get up Heath Street, and it made him rather impatient with me, and when we did arrive at the fair, the music made me burst into tears. Fair music always had excited me and given me a kind of lump in my throat, but Charles did not get this feeling, so he said I was being even more stupid than usual, and if I felt like that I had better go home. Before we left he made a little drawing of the fair, seen from one of the little hills surrounding the Vale of Health. He was quite pleased with it and said he would bring his paints on Monday, but on Monday something happened to prevent this plan.

10

On Easter Sunday we had shepherd's pie for supper, and I felt rather sick afterwards and went to bed early. I usually slept alone in the bedroom now and Charles on the divan in the living-room. I couldn't shut the door properly, because there was only a handle on the outside. The knob on the inside had gone even before we came, but we did not like to mention it because we were behind with the rent so often.

I felt very tired and soon went to sleep, but was wakened later by the noise of a great wind that had come. The windows rattled and the door banged and my tummy ached quite a lot, so I thought it would be a good idea to go to the lavatory, but when I reached the door found it was jammed to; then, of course, I wanted to go to the lavatory twice as much. I had to call Charles and ask him to open the door from the outside. He was rather annoyed at being woken in the middle of the night, so I went sadly downstairs, but as I was leaving I noticed some blood on the floor, and felt quite sure it had come out of me, so remembering what it said on the instructions, I went and woke Charles again. He was really angry this time and said I was always imagining things, and even if it was the baby I would have to wait until the morning. I went back to bed feeling rather in disgrace. Before I went to sleep I remembered about the beastly door, so got out again and put a chair there so that it couldn't shut again. The door banged against the chair, the windows rattled even more fiercely, and everything was grim, but I dozed off eventually.

Then I awoke with a start and felt dreadfully frightened. I thought there must be a ghost in the room that had startled me, so I listened and I heard a queer little popping sound that seemed to come right out of me, and suddenly I was all flooding with water. I went to the living-room and wakened Charles again. I told him I was sorry to be such a bother all the time, but this time it really was serious. I'd grown so fat I had burst. He could see I wasn't imagining things this time, and he looked quite worried as he got out of bed. He said he would go out and get a taxi to take me to the hospital. Then he looked in his pockets and only found ninepence, so I told him about the five shillings in the case. When he opened the case, there was the pink card from the hospital saying I would not be admitted unless I was in labour. We didn't know if all this water was labour or not, but Charles said the hospital would have to admit me now I was all broken, so he went off to try to find a taxi.

When I was alone I began to feel dreadfully frit again, and my teeth chattered, but there was not quite so much water coming out of me now, so I went into the kitchen to boil a kettle so that I could wash myself, but suddenly a most enormous pain came and doubled me right up. Just at that moment the kettle which had a whistle in the spout started to boil and whistle away. I tried to get at it to stop the piercing shrieks it was making, but the pain was so fierce I could hardly move. At last it left me and I was able to throw the wretched whistle part of the kettle away; I never wanted to hear it again.

I quickly washed and dressed before another pain could get me, but my clothes became all messy and I had to dress all over again because I didn't want to be disgraced at the hospital. In spite of several attacks of pain I managed to dress, do my hair and even make up my face, but it was rather smudged because my hands shook so much.

When Charles returned, he was most relieved to see me looking almost normal, but he found it rather difficult getting me down three flights of stairs, because I had become all doubled up. When we had got in the taxi the pains began to come much quicker, but I discovered if I said 'Along the bridge Lord Marmion rode, etc.' very quickly over and over I could bear the pain much better, so I did this for the rest of the journey and it was a great help.

When we arrived at the hospital, we went down the familiar steps to the basement and found it all locked up, then we went up the steps and through the front door. The door man touched his hat and I felt proud, as if I had graduated to the sixth form. We spoke to an elderly nurse who appeared from somewhere, and I was taken to a dreary room with a lot of dark brown paint all over the place. I was given a bundle of hospital clothes and told to undress and fold my clothes up neatly for my husband to take home. I didn't like parting with my clothes. It made it seem so prison-like. I couldn't escape if I wanted to without any clothes.

The hospital clothes were a very poor exchange for mine. They were simply awful – a grey flannel shirt, pink cotton dressing gown, and some really frightful white cotton stockings. I tried to leave them off, but the elderly nurse appeared again and made me put them on. Then I had to lie down on a kind of bed arrangement and she brought Charles in to say goodbye. I felt so ashamed for him to see me wearing those ghastly clothes, and as soon as he saw me he started laughing and said, 'Darling, if you only knew how funny you look!' I did, and hoped I wouldn't die, in case he always remembered me like that. When he had finished laughing, he kissed me, and the nurse told him to come back in the morning. Then he had gone, and I felt dreadfully alone.

After he had gone, such a lot of things happened. I must have been in at least seven different wards and beds before the baby came. They kept me on the move all the time, and the only thing I wanted was to be left alone in privacy. I must have given up the famous pink card and been examined by a doctor, but I can't remember quite when that happened. The next thing to Charles leaving was being taken to a nice, tiled bathroom and being told to have a bath. In my hand was the suitcase with the teapot and clean night-dresses. When the nurse left I made several attempts to get in the bath, but I was so doubled up I couldn't manage it, so I just took off the hateful clothes and made some wet marks on the cork mat with my hands to make it appear as if I had had a bath. The nurse came back and caught me in this deception. She said I was a dirty woman to be afraid of water, and stayed in the room while I crawled into the bath. I was getting very discouraged by this time.

The next thing I can remember is walking behind a nurse and carrying my suitcase in my hand. We came to a room or ward with two nurses in it, and some rather high beds without sheets. There were not any people in the beds. I had to climb into one, and they asked me some questions and filled in forms. Every time I went into a new room this happened. When they had finished asking questions one of the nurses shaved me. This was a bit difficult, because the pains kept coming and it was difficult to keep still. When she had finished, she put very strong disinfectant on me. This smarted a lot, but it was almost a relief to have a different sort of pain. Then they gave me an enema, the first I had ever had, and it shamed me a lot, but the next thing they did was even worse – a large dose of castor oil which made me dreadfully sick for hours.

After this I escaped from the torture chamber and was taken to a room called the labour ward. There were other women there that had not actually started their labour yet, but were expected to have difficult confinements. They were talking quite cheerfully, and it made me feel better to hear them, because all the nurses had been so grumpy and impatient with me. I had begun to think it was a disgraceful wicked thing to do – to have a baby.

I lay in bed for about an hour and kept shivering. The pain did not seem quite so bad now I wasn't being disturbed all the time. Unfortunately, a maid came with some tea and bread and butter on a tray. I took one look and was sick all over the bed. The nurse in charge of the ward came and looked at me disgustedly and asked why I hadn't asked for a bowl to be sick in. I was taken out of the labour ward and put in another room, all by myself. I carried my horrid case, which appeared every time I was moved, although it disappeared each time I got into bed. Two nurses came and examined me. I heard one say it would be about two hours before the baby came. Two more hours seemed an awful long time. The pains got much worse again, and I tried saying 'Lord Marmion', but they told me to be quiet. I longed to cry out, but knew they would be angry, so bit my hands. There are still the scars on them now. My hands seemed to smell of Grapenuts and I remembered a white dog we used to have when we were children and she kept having puppies all the time – I felt very sorry for her now. They gave me a bowl to be sick in and I managed not to get any on the bed, but without any warning the wicked castor oil acted and I was completely disgraced. The nurse was so angry. She said I should set a good example and that I had disgusting habits. I just felt a great longing to die and escape, but instead I walked behind the disgusted nurse, all doubled up with shame and pain.

The next ward I went to had a toilet behind a curtain. There were other women in this ward and I did so hope I wouldn't disgrace myself again. As soon as the nurse left, I crawled behind the curtain. The pain was terrific now. It seemed like the end of the world, but I was determined I would not make the bed dirty again. There was just this great agony and a white curtain and a shining brass rail.

Suddenly it changed and I was on a kind of trolley. The next place I found myself was a brilliantly lighted room, with two doctors and a nurse. As soon as I arrived in the room I could tell they were going to be kind. I was lifted off the trolley on to a very high kind of bed-table arrangement. I looked round the room and saw there were two little cots, and in one was a baby that had just been born. I could hear it making queer little noises.

I explained to the nurse that I kept being sick all the time, but she didn't seem to mind. Every time I had a great pain she made me pull a twisted sheet that was fixed to the head of the bed in some way, and she would say, 'Bear down, Mother.' I tried to explain I wasn't a mother, but couldn't get it out. In between the pains they asked me questions so that they could fill in even more forms.

I looked for Dr Wombat, but he wasn't there. I did not mind, because the doctors that were there seemed kind and so was the nurse except that she kept hurrying me up. There was one dreadful thing – they made me put my legs in kind of slings that must have been attached to the ceiling; besides being very uncomfortable it made me feel dreadfully shamed and exposed. People would not dream of doing such a thing to an animal. I think the ideal way to have a baby would be in a dark, quiet room, all alone and not hurried. Perhaps your husband would be just outside the door in case you felt lonely. Once the baby had arrived I would not mind how many nurses and doctors came in attendance.

One of the doctors stood by my head and said he would give me something to put me to sleep in a minute, and the nurse kept urging me to bear down and I could feel everyone trying to hurry me up. Then I was enveloped in a terrific sea of pain, and I heard myself shouting in an awful, snoring kind of voice. Then they gave me something to smell and the pain dimmed a little. The pain started to grow again, but I didn't seem to mind. I suddenly felt so interested in what was happening. The baby was really coming now and there it was between my legs. I could feel it moving and there was a great tugging in my tummy where it was still attached to me. Then I heard it cry, so I knew it was alive and was able to relax. Perhaps I went to sleep. The next thing I knew was the doctor was pressing my tummy, but although it hurt, it didn't seem to matter.

I asked the nurse what kind of baby it was and if it was perfect. She said, of course it was, but I asked her to make sure it had all its fingers and toes. She laughed and said it was a lovely little boy, rather small, but quite healthy.

I couldn't help crying when I heard it was a boy, because I knew there wasn't much chance of Charles liking it, now it was a boy – he particularly disliked little boys. I longed to see the baby, but they said I couldn't yet. It had stopped crying and I was worried in case it was dead. So I cried about that, too.

11

I was being pushed along on a trolley again. There was my little case perched up on my toes. It seemed extraordinary it had not been lost during my travels. I was wheeled through some glass doors and found myself in the largest ward I had been in so far. There were ten beds, besides some emergency ones in the middle of the room. The third bed was empty, and I was put into it. The blankets were scarlet and over the bed was some large lettering saying the bed was endowed by New Zealand.

It was wonderful to be in bed and to know I was not going to be moved about any more, and all the pain was over. Outside in the street a barrel organ was playing 'Valencia' and inside I could hear the mothers chatting away to each other and a pretty ward-maid with red hair polished the floor with a heavy-looking buffer.

I lay dozing and feeling quite happy, the women chatting and nurses bustling about. All seemed far away, but after a time there was a new noise, a tinny clattery noise, and it was trays of lunch arriving. When I saw the dreary-looking boiled fish and watery rice pudding that was heading for me I said I didn't want any, but the nurse firmly insisted I must eat it even if I did not want to. I left as much as I dared, but the nurse came back with the tray and made me finish it. It felt like being at school again.

After lunch all the mothers had to have a sleep, and at two o'clock the babies were brought in to be fed. I so longed to see my baby, but they did not bring him to me. I asked the nurse when I could have him, and she said she would show him to me as soon as she was not so rushed. I began to worry and to think he was either deformed or black, but the nurse assured me he was a perfect baby and weighed six pounds. It seemed odd to have a son I had never seen. I was sure he was cold all by himself.

The nurse returned and put some more pillows under my head. I liked to lie almost flat, but she said all mothers in this hospital had to have masses of pillows, so that they were sitting up all the time. It drained them or something, but it was not at all comfortable, and made you feel tired behind. Every now and then a nurse would come and pull me up into a sitting position.

When there was another rattle of tin trays it was tea-time and they came and asked me if I had brought tea, butter, sugar and jam (it wasn't wartime). I said I hadn't any of those things, only a teapot, so they said I must tell my husband to bring them next time he came – it was a visiting night that day – that does not sound right. There were two visiting evenings a week just for husbands, and they could come on Sunday afternoon and bring a relation if they wished.

Then it was six o'clock and all the babies came out again – but not mine. This time I could not help crying. I was sure he was dead. I knew if you took a new-born puppy away from its mother it died quite soon. I felt positive my poor baby had died from loneliness and cold. They were taking them back now – the babies – they took them through the glass doors and through another door on the right. I planned as soon as the ward was empty of nurses I would creep out and find my cold poor baby. Then just as I thought the coast was clear, there was a nurse returning. Behind her was Charles. As soon as he came near I said, 'Oh, Charles, have you seen the baby? I know it is dead.' He said they would have told him if it was dead, and he didn't want to see it ever now it was a boy. I became so upset he went to the nurse and asked if he could see the baby. He looked awfully embarrassed.

When he returned he said there was an awfully nice baby rather like a Japanese, with lots of black hair. He said he wouldn't have minded that one so much, but ours was rather grim, very thin and red with red hair, and an awful look of himself about it. I asked if it felt cold and he said he hadn't touched it, although the nurse had tried to make him hold it. I was so glad to hear it was alive I did not mind how ugly it was, and if he looked like Charles he would be quite handsome.

Charles said he had borrowed some money to send telegrams to his relations saying we had a boy of six ounces. I told him it was six pounds not ounces, but he said a few pounds either way wouldn't make any difference. But Charles's telegrams caused a huge sensation, and his family was most disappointed when in due course they discovered we had had quite a normal baby.

I felt more easy in my mind now I knew the baby was alive, and later on, when they brought the babies in for their last feed that night, mine came with them. When the nurse gave him to me I just looked and looked at him, to make up for all the time I had missed. He was very like Charles, except for the red hair.

Charles was fair and my hair was almost black, so I can't think where the red hair came from. I thought he was the best baby I had ever seen. I looked at his little fingers and toes and they all had perfect nails. He even had eye-lashes; nothing had been forgotten. He was dressed in the most frightful clothes, a short flannel night-dress, all washed hard and yellow, and a piece of old blanket for a shawl, and a fragment of sheet for his napkin. He was just a rag-bag for old bed-clothes. His tiny feet were frozen and his hands, too; I held him to me to warm him. The nurse came and said I was to try to feed him, but he made grunting noises and would not wake up, so they took him away, and almost before he had left the ward, I had gone to sleep.

12

I left the hospital after nine days. The nine days were not very happy, but interesting. I liked to watch and listen to the other mothers. They were all working-class women. Some of them were very poor. In bed, with their hair hanging over their shoulders, they looked gentle and pretty, but when they dressed to go home they looked completely different. The older ones screwed their hair in untidy buns at the back of their heads, and their faces became all hard and haggard, their skirts hung down behind and their backs were bent and their poor feet had bunions. The young ones changed, too, when they were dressed. They did not look so shabby, but their faces were almost brazen. One was only sixteen. There was a little dark woman whose husband was a costermonger. She had had six children and they had all died at birth, now at last she had a living baby; but every time she fed it, it was sick, and it was discovered it had a kind of appendicitis. They operated on it and when I left the hospital it was recovering. I hoped very much it would not die.

My baby was beginning to grow very pretty, but was thin and delicate. He wasn't hungry like the other babies. He just went to sleep over his meals, but he never cried. Instead of growing, he became smaller and smaller, and now only weighed five pounds. This worried me immensely.

I asked Charles what he wanted the baby to be called, and after a little thought, he said 'Pablo', after Picasso, would be a good name. I thought 'Pablo' sounded rather impressive, but could imagine how tired one would get hearing people say 'Why do you call your baby Pablo? Is it a boy or a girl?' The other babies in the ward were all called Maureen, if they were girls, and Peter and John for the boys. They called mine 'Ginger', which I did not like very much.

Next time Charles came he suggested Sandro and Augustus. I was so happy he was taking an interest in the baby, I did not want to hurt his feelings, although I didn't like any of these names much. I felt you couldn't call a tiny thing that grew smaller every day Augustus, so I said it had better be Sandro. The next day a registrar visited the hospital and the mothers who had chosen their children's names had them registered, so I had mine registered Sandro Thomas Hardy Fairclough. I added Thomas Hardy because he was my favourite author at the time. I was not sure if Charles expected Botticelli after Sandro or not, but left it out because of spelling difficulties.

When Charles came to visit me on Sunday, he brought Eva with him. She was staying at our flat. I guessed she must have found it in an awful mess, but Charles said the mess was much worse after she left – the sink had blocked and had overflowed all over the kitchen floor and the saucepans were burnt and there had been another row about the bathroom. Eva was most interested to see the baby, but detested the name Sandro and was shocked at the dreary, rather smelly clothes he was wearing.

I was glad I was dressed in my own night-dress, not the evil grey shirt. I had had to keep it on for twenty-four hours, and it had been all covered in blood and horrible.

Eva was quite kind on this visit and gave me some grapes and flowers, the first I had had. All the same, I hoped she would have left the flat before I came home, but I rather thought she would not put up with the discomfort for more than a weekend, and in this I was quite right.

The nine days before my return home passed very quickly, I suppose because they were all more or less the same. The red-letter days were the ones we had visitors. If Charles was late and part of the visiting time was wasted, I would cry with disappointment, but he always came in the end. Sometimes he brought Ann with him. She liked to see the baby – her first nephew, but was inclined to make remarks about the other visitors. She seemed to think they were deaf.

The other excitement was the morning post, but I did not receive many letters. One came from Paul saying he was glad I had had a son to carry on the family name. I turned the envelope inside out to see if there was a cheque that had been mislaid, but it was empty. There was a letter from my brother John's wife, renewing my invitation to visit them when I had recovered.

The day started at five, when they used to bring the babies in for their first feed, and ended at eleven, for their last meal. Although that sounds a long day, it really passed very quickly. It was not very pleasant being woken up so early in the morning, but there were other things I disliked much more. The worst thing of all was the dirty bed linen and general roughness. The food was very poor, too. All they provided for breakfast and tea was three thick slices of bread and hot water for the tea and a jug of milk. Charles had brought in a packet of tea but he had no money to buy me butter and eggs and jam and things like that, so I just had to eat the dry bread. We did get two pounds from the insurance people I had been insured with when I had worked in the studio, but we had to give the hospital that. I can't help feeling if we are all the King's subjects the least he or the Government could do is to pay our birth expenses.

The day before we left the hospital, we had an examination by a doctor. The old mothers said this was a most painful and dreadful examination, and we all dreaded it, but as a matter of fact, it hardly hurt at all. After that we would get up and help in the ward a little, and the nurses were supposed to give the mothers a lesson in bathing the baby. But they were usually much too busy to do this.

The day of going home was almost as exciting as the last day of the school term. There was a certain amount of anxiety in case your husband did not bring the right clothes for yourself and baby; otherwise all was happiness. The proper procedure, after you had had a bath and dressed to go home, was to return to the ward carrying the baby in its best flowing robes and a large lace veil over its face, then go to each bed and say goodbye and show the baby in all its splendour. When it was my turn to leave the thought of doing this made me feel awfully shy. But when the nurse came to dress Sandro it was discovered Charles had brought three vests and two white petticoats and no frock; he didn't look very grand, so I solved the problem by standing at the ward door and shouting Goodbye and leaving very quickly.

The Austrian woman artist had sent a large hired car to take me home and I felt very grand and happy to be going home again. Charles seemed pleased to be with me, but kept looking at the baby with disgust. He said the thing that made him dislike it most was the resemblance to himself.

When we arrived home the first thing I noticed as we came up the stairs was the frightful smell of fish, and when we reached the living-room I saw the reason. Charles was in the middle of painting a picture of some herrings on a newspaper, and they had gone most high. He said they must not be thrown away until he had finished the painting. Already they had changed colour considerably, so we had to sit in the bedroom, and you could still smell them there.

Charles made me some tea. He said he had got quite used to doing things for himself while I had been away. The flat was in a beastly state. I noticed when he opened the food cupboard there was a pink blancmange I had made before I went away, but it had gone green now. I tried not to notice any of these things, because I didn't want Charles to think I was all womanly and fussy and how peaceful it was without me.

During the next few days people kept calling to see the baby. I think they must have thought I had had a mermaid instead of a baby – the smell of fish was so strong. The old woman with the twisted hands came and she said, 'He looks a very poor baby to me. You should take him to a clinic,' and she sniffed reproachfully.

As a matter of fact, Sandro had improved a little since he came home. He didn't behave like a dormouse at meal-times any more. But in spite of this slight improvement I was very afraid he would die. I kept looking in his cot every few minutes; even in the night I had to do this to make sure he hadn't died. The first bath I gave him was simply terrifying. His head wobbled about so, I thought it would fall off, but it didn't, and in a few days he loved me bathing him and would kick and stretch himself in the water.

Now Sandro was eating better he was often sick after I'd fed him and I felt rather alarmed in case he had an appendicitis. Then I recalled what the old woman had said about a clinic and thought maybe it would be a good thing to take Sandro to one, so I asked several motherly-looking women with prams if there was one near and they told me the nearest one and the time to go. So the next Wednesday at two-thirty I went. I knew it was the right place as soon as I drew near. You could hear the babies screaming, and there was a mass of hooded prams at the door. Some of them smelt. I went upstairs to the room all the noise was coming from. It was a large, dreary room, rather dirty. I had expected everything to be white and bright posters on the walls of children drinking milk or playing in the sun, but it was not like that at all. There were about twenty-five mothers and their children, and several middle-aged helpers. None of the windows were open. The helpers gave me a great welcome and soon I was sitting on a low chair waiting to have Sandro weighed. Most of the babies were healthy and clean and nicely dressed, but there were a few sickly-looking, dirty ones. I saw one of these drop its dummy, and the mother, a toothless old hag, picked it up from the floor and put it in her own mouth to clean it, and gave it back to the green-faced baby.

After Sandro was weighed I had to wait to see the doctor. The doctor was a woman. The other mothers did not like her much, perhaps because she was very quiet and firm and not in the least gushing, but I found her very helpful. She said the reason Sandro was so sick was that he was overfed at each meal, and she gave me quite a lot of good advice and put some plaster on his tummy because his navel stuck out too much and told me to bring him to see her again in a month's time. When their babies had been seen to mothers could have a cup of tea and a bun in the basement if they liked, but I was too scared of the matey heartiness of the helpers to do this. After this first visit I took Sandro to the clinic nearly every week. I felt the advantages outweighed the disadvantages. Charles was very scornful of the whole business.

Charles still disliked him, but in spite of this made some drawings of us together, so I hoped eventually he would get used to him. At the moment I felt I had most unreasonably brought some awful animal home, and that I was in disgrace for not taking it back to the shop where it came from.

13

We had no money at all and the milkman wouldn't leave any milk because we hadn't given him any money lately. He was quite nice about it and said we could have some free milk every day if we applied to the council. Mothers with new babies were allowed one pint a day if they had no money. The council went up in my estimation when I heard about this. Up till now I had thought it was almost a criminal offence to have a baby. All the same I did not apply for the free milk, because I was afraid they would take the baby away and put it in a home on the grounds of its parents having no visible means of support.

To my great relief the artist I had been sitting for before Sandro was born wrote and asked me to sit for him with the baby. He wanted to start the painting right away if I was well enough to pose. So I went the very morning the letter arrived. I was still feeling rather weak – Sandro was only two or three weeks old – and I found the long bus journey to Chelsea rather trying. I had a stupid idea you had to take babies upstairs in buses, like dogs, and this made travelling more difficult, but when I once arrived at the studio I did not find the posing trying. It was a joy to sit down and collect my strength for the journey home. On the return journey Sandro was sick right into a woman's umbrella. It wasn't a rolled-up one.

Fortunately, the picture took some time to paint, so we did not have to worry about money so much. And when it was finished Edmund called and said he was going to Leamington on business by car and offered to take me to my brother John's house, which was on his way. I felt rather guilty leaving Charles with only seven-shillings-and-sixpence. But I was feeling so tired, the thought of getting away from London and having plenty to eat seemed like heaven, so I sent a telegram to my brother and the next day Edmund called for me in his car. To my dismay it was an open sports model and I thought poor little Sandro would die from draught, but happily when he arrived at my brother's house he was still alive, very hungry and wet.

After a few days in the country he started to grow – you could almost see him doing it – and I felt better, too. John, my brother, and his wife had no children. They were careful people and said they could not risk having a family in case John died or lost his job. He had had the same one for fourteen years. They said only people with private incomes should have children. Perhaps they were right.

John's wife was called Joyce and she was very kind in a sensible, unimaginative way. She knitted Sandro some warm, rather stiff garments, and she gave me two of her frocks to wear – they had no shape in them and were fawn. She also gave me some lisle stockings and said I mustn't wear bare legs while I was staying with them. This made me a bit sad. I wouldn't have minded so much if they had been silk stockings she had given me, but she said it was common to wear silk stockings in the country.

She did not like lipstick either, and asked me not to wear it during my visit, or the little gold rings I always wore in my ears. I felt very colourless and dull, but it was worth it to see how Sandro was improving. He lived in a clothes-basket in the garden all day, under an apple tree covered in blossom. One day a bird made a mess on his head and the old cook said it was a lucky omen. He hardly ever cried.

I wanted to write to Charles, but had no money for a stamp, so I wrote a letter and made a sticky mark on the envelope, to look as if the stamp had come off in the post. It was difficult having no money. I began to need things for the baby – cotton-wool and baby-soap and powder. Joyce would say, 'I am going shopping in Leamington, is there anything you need for Sandro?' And I would say, 'Oh no,' then the next morning when he was having his bath she would see I had no powder.

After we had been staying there three weeks, they started to say, 'How is Charles? He must miss you,' or 'It has been nice having you to stay!' so I knew they were expecting me to leave. I was beginning to miss Charles and would have been quite glad to go home, but had no money to get there. I wrote Edmund an unstamped letter (I didn't bother to make a sticky mark for him) and asked him to take me back to London. He wrote back and said he would be passing that way again in a week and would gladly take me home again. So I told Joyce and I could see she was awfully relieved. I think they thought I was so comfortable I would just stay and never go home again.

At the end of a week I packed all our things to be ready in case Edmund sent a telegram to say he was coming, but nothing happened and John and Joyce began to exchange glances, and they would ask me at breakfast if I had had any letters. One morning Joyce said, 'Poor Charles, he has been on his own for over a month now. Are you sure you haven't quarrelled?'

After this I wrote Charles another letter, asking him to borrow enough money for me to return to London, but he wrote in return he had been so poor he had sold the rocking-chair and pawned the silver teapot. Another week passed and I felt so dreadfully I had outstayed my welcome. They never said outright, 'When on earth are you going?' but made remarks about spring-cleaning the spare room after I had gone. I tried to ask them for a little money to go home with – I only needed about fifteen shillings – but I did not want them to know how poor we were, they would have been so shocked. John was one of these nervy people who hate knowing the truth. Sometimes when he returned in the evening he would say to his wife, 'Has anything awful happened while I've been away? If it has, please don't tell me about it.'

I suddenly thought the only thing to do would be to walk back. It was only one hundred miles and I would surely get a lift part of the way. So I packed all our clothes again and wrote a little note asking them to be sent G.W.R. C.O.D. I just left out a few nappies to change on the way. I planned to leave the next morning very early and take a loaf and two oranges to eat on the way. When I had finished packing the gong went for dinner and I ran downstairs feeling quite happy and determined to eat a good meal that would last a long time. When I reached the bottom of the stairs the maid was asking someone into the drawing-room and it was Edmund. He said he was in a great hurry, but if I could be ready in five minutes he would take me back to London with him, so I didn't wait for dinner, but bundled Sandro into a shawl and got in the car. John and Joyce kept saying it was very odd to leave at that time of night, but they were so glad I was really leaving they did not protest too much.

14

The summer came and passed. Sometimes we were happy
and spent days in the sun on the Heath. Sandro was very
little trouble. He ate and slept and played with his toes until I
bought him a rattle, then he played with that. I fed him myself,
so he hardly cost anything to keep. He was still rather small, but
very healthy. His hair was a golden red and very curly and his
skin was brown, and his eyes a very dark brown.

We had very little money that summer, but Charles did sell
a few designs for book jackets and I went on sitting for artists.
Usually they did not want me to pose with the baby, so I had to
leave him behind with Charles and rush back at lunch-time to
feed him. Charles learnt how to change nappies and did not
seem to resent him quite so much. Sometimes he even seemed
to be amused by him. But just when I began to feel more hopeful that in time Charles would grow really fond of Sandro
something happened which upset and hurt me dreadfully. He
got in touch with one of his father's unmarried sisters and asked
her to find particulars of how to have Sandro put in a home for
children whose parents could not afford to keep them. The aunt

wrote me a long letter saying she would gladly see to all the arrangements and I must give up my baby for Charles's sake. I could earn much more if I was not tied to a baby and I must not get lazy. It was not fair to expect Charles at his age to support a wife and child. The letter was such a shock. I'd saved it up till I'd finished breakfast, because I so seldom received a letter and thought it might be something nice. When I opened and read it, I couldn't help thinking of Charles and his family as monsters who wanted to take my baby away and I felt I could never trust Charles again.

I had an appointment to sit that morning to an elderly artist who loved to paint girls in kimonos and dressing gowns slightly open in front, but I dared not leave Sandro in Charles's care in case he was gone when I returned, so I ran out to the nearest telephone box and said I would be unable to come for a few days. Charles was in bed when I showed him his aunt's letter. He was rather scared lying in bed with me standing over him storming away. He said: 'Babies have no feelings and would be just as happy in an orphanage as anywhere else.' On the other hand, he would be much happier if the baby was out of the way, so to send him to a 'home' was much the most reasonable thing to do. I just hated Charles then. I told him I wasn't going to work any more, but stay at home and guard Sandro, but he said that was quite unnecessary, because if I felt about the matter so strongly he would write and tell his aunt. There was nothing to make such a fuss about . . .

For three days I stayed at home and we had no money, and after the first day, no food and no shillings to put in the gas meter, so we couldn't even make a cup of tea, and, what Charles minded most, no cigarettes. We hardly spoke to each other, and

71

by the third day he had grown quite humble and sad. Maybe it was hunger made him get that way, but whatever it was, I felt I could trust Sandro with him, so I walked down to the elderly painter of girls in dressing gowns and told him I'd be able to sit for him the next day and would he lend me fourpence-half-penny. I bought a loaf with this on the way home; it was hot and new, and I pulled bits of crust off and ate them on the way. When I got home we cut the remains of the loaf in half and we ate it and felt all heavy afterwards.

Then the autumn came and I got quite a lot of employment in Art Schools and Sandro had grown so pretty some advertising studios photographed him for advertisements for patent foods which he had never had. They paid a guinea for each photograph. I only got seven-and-six a morning for being an artist's model. One school that gave me a lot of work was chiefly patronised by very well-to-do girls. In the rest-times the model was expected to sit in a tiny cell, smaller than a lavatory, so that she could not contaminate the young ladies. The walls of the cell were covered in rude remarks the models had written in pencil about the students and school. Sometimes the girls would ask me to pose at their homes on Sunday. They lived in places like Roehampton and Richmond and the fares were expensive. It was too far to come home for lunch, so they used to provide that. I had to eat it all by myself in the morning-room and I used to think how horrible amateur artists were compared to real ones.

With all these sittings (that sounds rather like a hen) we did fairly well the first half of the winter; at least we had enough to pay for our food and rent, which was the main thing, and some-times we had some over for coal, too. Then Christmas came and we decided it was too complicated to travel with a baby and it would be nice to have a Christmas at home.

People suddenly became very kind. Even Charles's family sent some packing-cases full of exciting provisions, and an American artist I had sat for sent a huge turkey and five separate shillings to pay for the cooking. A registered letter came addressed to me, and when I opened it there was five pounds inside. It didn't say who it was from, but it quite made our Christmas. So with all these nice things happening we had a lovely Christmas. We had no visitors. Ann was staying with my brother and Francis and James had gone to their families. I cooked the dinner very nicely, and we had crackers and all the proper Christmas things. Sandro sat at the table in his new high chair, which Francis and his sister had given him, and we even had wine – Paul had sent a bottle. There was a tree for Sandro, simply covered in coloured glass balls, and toys, too. He already had a stocking full that morning. He couldn't quite make out what they were, but thought they were very funny and kept laughing. He loved the crackers and the candles when we lit them on the tree. That was the best Christmas we ever had.

After Christmas things became grim again. No more book jackets came Charles's way and my model work was irregular and poorly paid, and the expenses were heavier now Sandro was weaned. We seldom had a fire and the light got cut off because we had not paid the bill, so we bought a little lamp for two-shillings-and-elevenpence and it gave quite a pretty light. We went to the electric light people and asked for the money we had given for a deposit back. It was nice to think they owed us money instead of it being the other way round. They gave us back the deposit money less what we owed them and it paid for our food for a week. These days we lived on vegetable soup and bread. Sandro had milk and an occasional egg as well.

Eva came to stay once during this bad patch, fortunately before we had the light cut off. Charles pawned an old-fashioned necklace of my mother's – it was the only piece of jewellery I had. It was worth losing it to hide the fact of the bad state we were in, but what I hated about pawning things was we never got them out again.

This was the first visit Eva had paid us since Sandro was born, and she was full of advice on how to bring him up. Apparently her children had completely given up nappies at six months, and had cut most of their teeth and were walking about at that age, so Sandro at nearly a year seemed very backward in comparison. She brought him a white crêpe-de-Chine suit with tiny frills. It was very grand, but when I washed it I couldn't get the frills to go back properly and she was disgusted when she saw it on her next visit. After that, when she gave me expensive clothes, I only let him wear them when she was there, so they showed hardly any signs of wear.

Sandro was rather backward walking, but he used to shoot about the floor on his bottom, propelling himself with his feet, and when he was put on his pot he used to skate about on that. He found this such a successful way of following me around, it was difficult to get him interested in walking. I used to worry in case he always went about like that. Otherwise, he was not backward at all and was very forward with talking and took a lively interest in everything we did, and almost never cried.

15

As the year went on our poverty got worse and worse. Charles just painted away and didn't notice unless there was no money for cigarettes. Then he would borrow a few shillings from Francis to buy some and he would be happy again. I was out working so much he had to look after Sandro nearly every day, but he was more reconciled to him now. If it was fine he would load the pram with painting materials and go up to the Heath for the day; if he worked at home he would give Sandro an old canvas, a brush and some paint, and he would sit down and paint very carefully until the canvas was quite covered and give no trouble at all.

When it was his first birthday I made a sponge cake with white icing and one candle in the middle. I had saved a few shillings and bought some cheap toys, too. Among them was a very large celluloid goldfish and he promptly ate the tail off when it was given to him on his birthday morning. The other toys I saved until the birthday tea.

For some reason this first birthday meant an awful lot to me. I was longing to see Sandro's delight in the cake and toys. When he was excited he would whistle through his two front teeth – he only had four. Unfortunately, I was sitting in a school that day so had to rush off after breakfast. If it had not been a school I was working for I would have cancelled it, because I had been so looking forward to this day. As it was I put the birthday tea and toys all ready on a tray and told Charles on no account was he to start before I returned at about four-thirty.

After the day's work I hurried home so fast I lost a little red cap I had been posing in, and the students were annoyed the next day when I arrived without it. They had to change all their paintings. But the cap was sacrificed in vain, because when I reached home there was no Sandro or Charles. I waited and waited until it was five o'clock, then six o'clock, then seven o'clock. By this time I was quite sure there had been a frightful accident. I even braved the landlady and went down and asked if anything awful had happened, and she said it very likely had but she hadn't heard about it yet.

Just as I had climbed the three flights of stairs, I heard Charles come in, so I rushed down again and there was Sandro asleep in the pram under a mountain of painting materials. I carried him upstairs. He was so sleepy he only woke up for a cup of milk and stayed asleep all the time I was undressing him, so it was no good having a birthday tea now. When I returned to the living-room, Charles had propped his painting up against the wall and was standing looking at it most intently. He was eating something, and when I looked closer it was the birthday cake; it was all cut and spoilt and Sandro had never seen it. The painting was of the beautiful church in Church Row, Old Hampstead. I'd always loved that church, but now I felt I hated it, and for months every time I passed that way, I wouldn't look at it.

76

After the birthday disappointment I became more and more discontented with our way of living. I disliked the flat and the depressing road we lived in. I felt we were getting like it. We had lost most of our friends now and we never went to a theatre, film or party. It was over a year since we had been out at all, even to tea. I could see how dreary our life was compared to the students in the schools I sat in. Sometimes the artists I sat for asked me to come to a party, but I never could, because of leaving Sandro at night. I couldn't expect Charles to look after him while I went out enjoying myself. Charles had got in such a rut he hardly knew he was alive. He never sold any paintings, because no one ever saw them. A few weeks after they were painted he reversed the canvas and painted on the other side, then if there was no money to buy a new canvas, he would scrape the last painting off and start a new one. All this seemed to have no beginning or end.

While I was posing I would try to make new plans to improve our lives. I came to the conclusion that the first thing we must do was move, move to a more accessible flat where Charles could have a proper studio and where we could entertain a little. I tried to save some money towards this move, but it was quite impossible, although I felt that if once I found a suitable flat the money would appear.

I did not tell Charles my plans. I thought he would be frightened of a new move because he had had all the work of the last one. Also he was in such a dreary kind of haze these days he would not like the idea of being disturbed. Ann did not go to her office on Saturday morning, so she used to come to the house agents with me. We both adored going into empty houses and flats. There were often odds and ends left from the

77

last tenants. From just a few things one could picture exactly the kind of people they were. Some of the places the agents sent us to were simply frightful and others could have been nice, but were covered in dark brown paint and had stained glass windows. I think there must be far more dark brown paint and stained glass in West Hampstead than in any other place in the world.

On the fourth Saturday morning of our hunt we discovered quite a suitable flat on the hall floor of a large, rather battered house in Abbey Road. There were two simply enormous rooms and a tiny kitchen and hall. The bathroom and lavatory were down the passage in the main hall and had to be shared with two other flats; but to make up for this there was a house telephone. The telephone decided me and we went back to the agents and said we would have the flat, and I borrowed a pound from Ann to leave as a deposit. The rent was six pounds a month in advance.

When I broke the news to Charles that we were moving he was most dismayed. He said he couldn't bear the idea and didn't want to lose the view from the bedroom window, but I kept enticing him with the beautiful large room he would have to paint in, so he consented to come and see the flat, and when he did, he also saw the possibilities it held and agreed to have it. So we wrote to his father and said for practical business reasons we must move to a more convenient house and could he let us have twelve pounds for the first month's rent and expense of moving. The letter must have been a good one, because the money came by return, so we gave the landlady a week's notice and away we went. I was full of hope, as usual.

We had collected quite a lot of odd pieces of painted furniture during the two years we had been married. Whenever people had something they did not want they gave it to us and we painted it to match the rest of our stuff. Everything was a pale greenish blue, the kind of colour some swimming-pools are. So although the rooms were so large they did not look too bare, except for the floors, and we had nothing to put on the bedroom floor at all. For poor people the most difficult thing to provide is floor covering. Everything is so expensive, even lino. I have often wished people could put rushes or sand on their floor in these days. It would have cost pounds to make curtains to fit the large windows, so we just had nothing. Studios seldom have curtains in any case.

The kitchen was not so nice as I had thought at first. For one thing it was dark, and another bad thing was, when I went to open the window I found it opened into a garage and a great smell of oil and petrol came in, and when they started up cars the smoke and fumes were terrific. But the room Charles was using for a studio seemed wonderful after the pokey little attics we had been living in, and having a large room to paint in seemed to improve his pictures, and they did improve almost straight away. Perhaps it was because he had never been able to walk back from his work and see it from a distance before.

Having a telephone was a great help in my work. Previously the artists that needed me had to write. Now if they had a few odd hours or a sitter had let them down, they would 'phone and I could be there in half an hour. There was a bus stop just outside the house.

Francis had a studio quite near and whenever he wanted to try out a new technique in painting he would get me to sit for him. He said I was the only person who sat for him who didn't get offended if the painting turned out badly. Once one of his

79

windows got broken, so he put an old canvas in its place to keep the draught out. It was an unsuccessful painting of me, and looked so reproachfully at me every time I passed in a 53 bus that I had to ask him to take it down.

Seeing so much of Francis did Charles good. They would talk about painting together for hours. When we had no money for food he would give us lunch. It was always the same lunch – scrambled eggs, tinned peas and carrots and a lot of coffee. He said he had an account with a grocer's shop and even if he had no money for several weeks he could still buy food, and by the time the bill had grown rather large some money always turned up.

We thought that was the best idea we had heard for a long time, so he took us to his grocer and said we wanted an account, and the grocer said we could have one, and it was lovely having an account like that. The grocer even had beer and when we had no money we would 'phone for some food and a bottle of beer and it was delivered to the door.

16

Soon we began to make new friends and were asked to parties, so we arranged with a married couple who lived on the same floor that we would keep an ear on their child when they went out if they would do the same for us. This worked quite well and made a great difference to our lives. Sometimes now Charles sold a painting to one of our new friends. This did not happen very often, but it did Charles so much good.

One party we went to was given by a drunken Australian artist who had a dank studio in St John's Wood. We arrived there rather late and nearly everyone was quite drunk and it was all very sordid. I wandered round looking at the sculpture, which wasn't much good. I'd always longed to model in clay, but could never afford to buy the necessary materials. I discovered a large bin of clay and on a sculptor's easel some fascinating tools. Hanging from a nail on a door was a dirty towel. I suddenly found myself pulling great lumps of clay out of the bin, and putting it in the towel. When I'd scooped out about half a hundredweight I added some of the tools. When I had made the towel into a bundle, I told Charles what I had done and he agreed to help me carry it home, so we crept out of the door that had had the towel hanging from it, and discovered ourselves in the garden. It was stiff with loving couples, but we managed to reach the road without treading on any. When we got outside we laughed and laughed; the bundle was so heavy, but we managed to get it home, laughing most of the way.

The next day I started modelling in clay. I had no armature, but made a substitute with some of Sandro's toys. He was most annoyed about this and became very red in the face and kept muttering to himself and pointing to the bust I was modelling. After this I spent all my spare time modelling. One bust was most successful. I did the nude body and neck from myself, but made up the head because I was too shy to ask anyone I knew to sit. I didn't like people to watch while I was working. The face was rather Burmese and I left the eye sockets hollow, which sounds gruesome, but, in fact, was most effective. The figure ended at the waist and I kept it wrapped in a nice piece of rubber sheeting. It had to be damped every day. I hoped to find someone who would help me cast it in plaster before it got too hard.

One evening when I'd gone to bed quite early, a sculptor who had seen a painting someone had done of me 'phoned and asked me to sit for him. Although we had not met, we had a long, friendly conversation. Then he said he knew I was beautiful by my voice. I didn't know what to say about that and rang off. Afterwards I regretted this, because we had made no arrangements about the sittings.

About half an hour later there was a great ringing of the bell and knocking of the door, so Charles went and found a sculptor – not the one I had stolen clay from, but the one who had 'phoned. I was ashamed to be in bed and have no lipstick on, but was glad the sheets were clean. This sculptor (he was called Bumble Blunderbore) was an enormous man, rather like Chesterton to look at, and he kind of wheezed when he breathed. I think it is hardened arteries that makes people do that. He was carrying two large bottles of what I thought was beer, but it turned out to be champagne. He said he had come to arrange about me sitting for him. Then he opened the champagne and we all sat on my bed, which was a divan, and drank it. It was the first I had ever had and made me feel so happy.

Then he walked round the room and looked at Charles's paintings and drawings. There was a small framed drawing of a woman's head and he said, 'How much do you want for that? Would a fiver do?' And when Charles said Yes, he wrote out a cheque straight away. Then he saw my clay bust and said it had 'great quality' and he offered to take it away in his car and get it cast. All this seemed like heaven and a fairy godmother and Christmas all in one. When the champagne was all gone he left, but it was arranged I should sit for him the next day, and he would come and fetch me in his car. When he had gone we felt very flat and sleepy.

The next day Charles left the house early. He was spending the weekend with James and his family, who had a little house in the New Forest. He cashed Bumble Blunderbore's cheque at the grocer's on the way to the station. We were worried in case he changed his mind when he looked at the drawing the next morning. Soon after Charles had gone, Bumble 'phoned and asked me to meet him at the Café Royal for lunch, and I said I would, but remembered afterwards there was no one to give Sandro his lunch now Charles was away, but eventually found someone in the house who was willing to do this. Then there was the problem of clothes. The only summer dresses I had were cotton ones I had made myself. They were all the same design, very tight in the bodice, with long, gathered skirts. I used to starch them a lot to make the skirts stick out. He hadn't seen me dressed yet, so I hoped he wouldn't think I was frightful when he did.

I was to meet him in the small private bar at the back of the restaurant. I had not been in a bar before and did not like to go in by myself, but I looked through the glass doors and saw him bulging over a round stool, looking rather like a bored Humpty Dumpty. When I went in he seemed very pleased to see me and asked what I would like to drink. I did not know so he said I had better have a Pimms Number One, and I was most impressed with all the things floating in the glass. Then a waiter came in and he ordered lunch – petit marmite soup, sole with mushroom sauce, chicken and ice cream: that is what he ordered. When all this was ready the waiter came back and led us to a table with Reserved written on it.

We sat over our lunch a long time and I found it was quite easy to chatter away to him, partly because of the drinks and because he was so appreciative. I told him Charles was away and he said his wife was away, too, so I must spend the weekend at his house in Maidenhead. He had a studio in London, too. I said I couldn't possibly do that because of Sandro, and he was most amused at the idea of me having a son and said he must come, too. Then I remembered his wife and suggested she wouldn't like strange women and children coming while she was away, but he said she was a 'great woman' and would be delighted; he had a daughter at school and she was a 'great woman', too.

So I agreed to go, but felt it would be a very difficult weekend with a baby in a strange house with no woman in it, and perhaps no proper meals or anything, but did not like to refuse and be ungrateful after eating all that lunch.

We went back to Abbey Road to pick up Sandro and a few clothes, and headed for Maidenhead. Sandro was delighted with the car ride. Bumble stopped at a cake shop and bought masses of disgusting cakes all covered in imitation cream and jam and gave him them to eat. Fortunately, he didn't like them, but thought it a good idea to smear them all over the seat and window of the car. Still, it would have made even more mess if he had been sick.

We were all rather sticky when we reached the house, which was Georgian and simply covered in wisteria. It was nice inside, too, but the furniture was most unsuitable – all sorts of periods and styles all jumbled up, and some of the rooms had frightful gold-embossed wallpaper. I was glad to see there was a servant. She showed me the spare room and did not appear at all surprised at my unexpected appearance. I asked her for some milk for Sandro, and when she had gone to fetch it Bumble came in with a large doll's cot for him to sleep in, so I put him to bed in that and he seemed quite happy.

When he had gone to sleep I went downstairs and there was another man with Bumble. He was big and fat, too, but didn't wheeze when he breathed. We had a cold supper which was already laid in the dining-room and afterwards we went out to a little pub by the river. It was the kind of place where everyone knew each other, and the barmaid was a 'great woman'. Bumble introduced me to everyone and told them he was going to start sculpting me the next day and it was going to be the best thing he had ever done, and I had a lot to drink and began to think perhaps I was rather beautiful and wonderful, but hadn't realised it before.

The next morning I awoke late when the maid came in with some tea. She also had some breakfast for Sandro. When we eventually came downstairs Bumble was working in the studio, still wearing his pyjamas. He said he would be ready for me to sit in about half-an-hour, so I routed round the house and found some toys to keep Sandro quiet and put him out on the lawn in his play pen which I had had the foresight to bring.

When I had fixed him up safely I returned to the studio and started to pose. Even after the first sitting the clay started to look interesting. I spent most of the day and some of the evening sitting and Sandro was as good as gold. I went home on Monday morning. Bumble hoped to finish the model the next weekend. I was rather doubtful if Charles would want me to come, but I had been given two pounds for my work and I thought he wouldn't mind being left alone if I earned another two pounds.

17

When Charles came back from the New Forest I told him all about my weekend. He was rather surprised, but made no objection to me going there again the next weekend, so I told Bumble when he 'phoned that I could come. After this I often went to Maidenhead, sometimes taking Sandro and other times by myself. Each time I went Bumble started a new head of me, and the next time I went it had all dried up or he would be bored with it. He would start another and say it was the best thing he had ever done, and I would get all excited about it, but nothing was ever finished.

This happened so often that eventually it became a farce me sitting and I gave it up. All the same, we were very good friends and I often stayed at his house. His wife seemed quite pleased to have me. She was a pleasant, sleepy woman who took everything as it came, even me. When Bumble was sculpting someone in his London studio he would often ask me to come and make tea and keep them amused. Sometimes they were grave, intelligent men he was sculpting, and I'm sure they did not find me in the least amusing, but were too polite to say so.

That first summer in Abbey Road was the happiest and most carefree time I ever had. Our own acute money troubles seemed to be a thing of the past. Bumble Blunderbore put quite a lot of work in Charles's way, but in the autumn he went to New York to have a one-man show. He stayed away for six months and when he returned he had rather forgotten us, although he did ask us to some rather grand parties.

We gave some parties, too, but ours were bottle parties. We used to get a few bottles of beer, and perhaps gin, to start things off, but everyone brought something. I loved giving parties, and preparing the sandwiches and arranging the flowers. Sometimes Charles would paint frescoes on detail paper and hang them up on our walls, and it gave a very good atmosphere. Charles was very clever at things like that. He was a good host, too, when he had had something to drink.

One evening a man we had recently met at Francis's studio asked us to dinner. His wife was away and he was the kind of man who thinks he can cook. Men are often like that. They say they can cook and it turns out to be an omelette, scrambled egg or sausages. They never can cook jam or Christmas pudding and proper things like that (I don't, of course, include chefs when I say this, I mean real men).

We had to meet our host in the foyer of a theatre for some reason, perhaps he had been to a matinée. All the people came surging out and there was our host accompanied by a tall, dark, sinister man, who looked as if he might be a Warlock; but when we were introduced to him his face looked quite different when he smiled, and he put all his parcels on the ground so that he could shake hands with me. His name was Peregrine Narrow. I don't think I have mentioned our host's name yet. It was Mr

Karam. He was a kind of foreigner, but I can't remember which kind. He hustled us all into an underground train and in due course we emerged at Belsize Park and went to his flat, which was simply stiff with Chinese Buddhas and goddesses of Mercy; Kuanyin, I believe they are called. That is how he lived – selling Chinese works of art to art dealers. They were most impressive, all those calm figures, but one couldn't breathe very well, there were so many. He asked me to help him in the kitchen and I was disappointed, because I wanted to talk to the sinister man, but consoled myself by the thought I could ask Mr Karam all about him while I worked.

As I expected, it was sausages, nasty, long, thin, German ones. There was some spaghetti, too, but nothing to make a sauce with, not even an onion, so I opened a tin of baked beans and grated a piece of dry cheese I found. It grated so fine I thought afterwards it must have been a knife handle. As I worked I asked Mr Karam to tell me Peregrine Narrow's life story, but he said all he knew about him was that he was divorced or separated from his wife and earned a living as art critic and journalist. He had also written one or two rather unsuccessful books on painting.

By the time I had learnt all this, in between washing up enough things for supper and the cooking, the meal was ready. It wasn't really a nice supper, except for the coffee, which was made by Mr Karam and was heavenly, but I enjoyed listening to Peregrine and looking at him as well. His dark face became full of animation when he talked (I think the right word to use for his face would be mobile), but when he was silent it became all bitter and sinister again, and his back was rather humpy. When I talked he listened most intently to every word I said, as if it was very precious. This had never happened to me before, and gave me great confidence in myself, but now I know from experience a lot of men listen like that, and it doesn't mean a thing; they are most likely thinking up a new way of getting out of paying their income-tax. Although he was quite old, forty-five, he asked me to call him by his Christian name, which suited him very well. I didn't like the Narrow part much. When he left he walked home with us and came in and saw Charles's paintings, which in the whole he seemed to approve of. My famous piece of sculpture had returned from the casters by this time and he suggested I sent it to an exhibition, and he picked out two of Charles's paintings that he thought might be accepted, too. When he left, he left his telephone number in case he could be of any use to us at any time. I put the telephone number in a safe place so that it wouldn't get mislaid.

18

As the winter came, that beastly poverty came, too. I had forgotten how sad it was being poor, and the rooms were so large we couldn't keep them warm at all. We still had our account at the grocers, but if we left the bill unpaid for over a month they wouldn't serve us, and if we left the rent unpaid an awful man in a bowler hat used to come. We still had our friends and were not lonely and cut off as we used to be, and I felt perhaps poverty this time was only temporary. Although Charles's paintings were improving all the time now, no one seemed to buy them, partly because he suddenly got the idea they were worth an awful lot of money. If anyone asked the price of a painting he would say it was fifty or even a hundred pounds, and hardly anyone we knew had as much money as that. We both had our work accepted in the mixed exhibition Peregrine had recommended us to send in to. I was very proud to see my sculpture mixed up with real sculptors' work; but we didn't sell anything.

I longed to spend more time sculpting now. A hundredweight of anonymous clay had arrived addressed to me, and I somehow felt it had been sent by Peregrine, but we hadn't seen him since that first meeting, so maybe I was quite wrong. I had suggested to Charles that we should 'phone him, but he said there wasn't anything to 'phone him about. I always asked after him when I met Mr Karam, who seemed to keep in constant touch with him, but I did want to meet him again. He had somehow taken my imagination.

Sandro resented my sculpting because it took my attention from him. He didn't whine and grizzle, but did naughty things. Once he found a sponge cake and a dozen eggs that had been left in the main hall for an old lady with a Peke. He arranged the eggs on the top of the cake and fetched a hammer and hammered them all into the cake. When they were well hammered in, he fetched me to see something 'pretty'. Another time when I was sculpting he threw all the teacups down the iron staircase that led to the garden. I rushed outside when I heard all the crashes, and told him how naughty he was, and for months afterwards whenever he saw broken glass and china on walls (I think it's meant to keep burglars away) he would say, 'Look, naughty.' He thought that was the official name for broken china.

He was growing so active Charles found it difficult to look after him while I was away from home working. He didn't sleep much in the daytime now and got very bored with being in the pram, and if he was left for long would unpick his knitted clothes, or pull the feathers out of the mattress; but if he was in the flat running about, Charles found it most difficult to work. I wished so much I could stay at home and look after him myself.

Then I had to stay at home because I caught 'flu; I think it was because it was so cold at home and in the studios where I used to work it was so hot and close I often used to faint. It was beastly having 'flu and not being able to earn any money. I had to live on Oxo cubes. Fortunately, I didn't give it to Charles and Sandro, so as soon as my temperature went down I was able to work again, but still felt rather wretched and fainted quite often and my periods went all wrong. I felt very tired because I had to sit on Sunday, too, to try to make up the money we had lost by me staying at home.

We both felt depressed about the wolf coming to the door again. We thought he had gone away for ever. Charles said the best thing we could do would be to have another party. We would just buy some beer to start with, and if everyone brought a bottle, we could take the empty ones to a pub and get quite a lot of money in return. So Charles drew some amusing invitations which we sent to our friends and we had a party. Lots of people came. Some of them we had never seen before, and some brought whole crates of beer. I painted the crates blue afterwards and used them for window-boxes. When all the people had come, I thought how nice it would be if Peregrine Narrow was there, too, so I went into the hall and 'phoned him. I was scared to because it was a long time since we had met him, and I thought he wouldn't remember who I was, but when I got through he said he would be delighted to come, so I went back to the party and didn't tell Charles. I hoped he would think he had come by accident.

He came very quickly in a taxi and it was a lovely party. Peregrine and Mr Karam stayed after everyone had gone, and we made tea and talked and talked; at least, the men talked; I just lay on the divan listening.

After that Peregrine often came to see us, and we went to his studio. I was disappointed in his paintings. They looked rather as if they had mud mixed in the paint, but I did not say so. I always felt the days we didn't see Peregrine were wasted.

19

Peregrine said he would like to paint a portrait of me. I didn't want to be painted looking all muddy, but thought it would be nice to sit in his studio and talk to him, and perhaps hear his life story, so I agreed to go twice a week. The painting started by being all little dabs of light colours, and I thought it looked rather promising, but gradually it grew more and more muddy, until it looked like Southend when the tide is out. All the same, I enjoyed going to his studio and, as I had hoped, heard a lot about Peregrine's previous life and marriage. He used to put his head in his hands and say how unhappy he was, and how he loathed his wife, who wouldn't divorce him. He talked about how horrible she was quite a lot, and I felt as if I would know her at once if I met her in the street.

They had married when he was twenty-one and his wife (who was called Mildred) was twenty-seven. She sounded the waddiest woman ever. He said she had a big chin and a large, flabby white face, and wore a lot of velvet and thought she was psychic. He said she simply smothered him, and after two years of married life he ran away. All these years he had been married to her, even before I was born, but still he couldn't get free. It was dreadful, and I felt so sad for him. Twice he had tried living with other women, but she had always found out, and used to arrive and make frightful scenes. He got so worked up when he talked about all this, his jaw would all tremble, and he would walk up and down and forget all about the painting, so it was no wonder he looked so bitter and sinister.

But when Peregrine wasn't thinking about his awful wife he was quite gay, and a charming companion. When my morning sitting was over he would take me to a restaurant to have lunch. I was proud of being seen lunching with a distinguished-looking, middle-aged man, except that sometimes people mistook him for my father, and he didn't like that very much. I used to eat a lot at these lunches, and sometimes when I got home I felt awfully sick.

I seemed to be feeling sick quite a lot lately, ever since I'd had 'flu. Then a great dread came in my mind, but I couldn't face it at first, but eventually I had to tell Charles I was awfully sorry but there seemed to be another baby coming. He was simply horrified and said he just couldn't bear the idea of any more babies, and I must do something to get rid of it. It wasn't fair to him to keep having children like this.

I was very scared about this idea – getting rid of babies – but there was still the chance it might be a mistake, so I went to a woman doctor who lived quite near. I'd seen her sometimes getting in and out of her car, and I thought she was nice. I asked her to examine me, and when she did she said there was a baby inside me, and it was nearly three months old. I told her all about Charles hating babies and how we depended on the money I earned. Then she asked me how I felt about having any more children and I told her I'd always hoped to have a simply enormous family, and although I couldn't help rather loving babies, I realised now it wasn't right to have a family unless you were rich. All the same, I didn't want to get rid of this one. It seemed a sordid and wicked thing to do. She said it was also a dangerous thing to do; then she offered to attend me and to bring the baby into the world for nothing. She was awfully kind, but said I must make Charles get a job, any job, even if it was nothing to do with painting.

I went home and told Charles all she had said, and he looked quite terrified and said he wouldn't give up his painting for beastly babies and ran out of the house. I felt all frightened, as if I'd done something wicked. I did wish it was the men sometimes that had babies. I would be awfully kind to Charles if he had one, although I would hate to see him looking all fat.

He didn't come back till late in the night, but I was still awake. He said he was sorry he had been so angry with me, but I must promise to get rid of this extra child. So I cried a bit and said I would as long as I didn't have to do anything too alarming.

The next morning Peregrine 'phoned to say he was going away for about six weeks on a lecture tour. He was excited about it, and said he would get in touch with me as soon as he returned. I was pleased he was going to be away now I felt so unhappy, because I knew men hate women when they are unhappy.

20

Charles kept asking people's advice on how to get rid of babies, and everyone seemed to know someone who knew someone who knew someone who did something which sounded quite crazy, like walking six miles carrying a heavy weight, or taking a dose of Epsom salts and swimming out to sea, or skipping for an hour. Someone's charwoman told him she used to drink a bottle of port mixed with quinine, and it never failed. I did try this, but it only made me sick for three days and the port was quite expensive, too.

Charles was getting desperate. I felt dreadfully sorry for him, but angry, too. Then the woman who lived at the top of the house, who already had two children, told me she had had an operation when she found she was going to have another. She said it had cost five pounds and the baby had gone away, but she was ill for three months after. She was a good woman and a very kind mother, but her husband had been out of work for a long time. It rather comforted me that even good women got rid of their babies, but I didn't like the idea of being ill for three months. I told Charles, in case he thought I should have that kind of operation, but I was very glad to hear that he didn't like the idea either.

Then he heard about a doctor who did illegal operations for twenty-five pounds. He said he had heard of several people who had been to him, and they hadn't died or been very ill or anything like that, so I agreed to visit this doctor if Charles would find the twenty-five pounds. I rather hoped he would be unable to raise such a large sum of money, but he went to five of our richer friends and told them we were behind with the rent and would be turned out if we didn't pay at once, and they all gave him five pounds; I did hope they didn't compare notes afterwards. Ann was one of the people he borrowed five pounds from, but she didn't know what it was for. We had kept this wretched baby a secret from her. She was the only person who we paid back. To throw away twenty-five pounds on this sordid operation seemed such a dreadful waste to me. I thought of all the lovely things we could have bought for the flat, or we could have had a holiday by the sea and some new clothes as well.

I don't feel much like writing about the actual operation. It was horrible and did not work at all as it should. I couldn't go to hospital, because we would have all gone to prison if I had. Even the doctor did his best to help me recover, although he was scared stiff to come near me when he saw it had all gone wrong, but eventually I became better. But my mind didn't recover at all. I felt all disgusted and that I had been cheated from having my baby. Now it had gone I wanted it more than ever; I felt I had been weak. I should have left Charles and had the baby somewhere. If I'd just become a tramp with Sandro surely someone would have taken us in, but instead of that I had murdered it.

While I had been ill Sandro had had to go away. He stayed with a married sister of Eva's who lived in the country. We did not, of course, tell them the truth about my illness. When I recovered and suggested bringing him home, they wrote and said he could stay there for a few months if we liked and share their child's nurse. They had a little girl of four and he would be a companion for her. Charles was very keen on this suggestion and I could hardly refuse to let him have a good country holiday with a trained nurse to look after him, instead of the very haphazard life he led with us, but I had an uneasy feeling about him being so far away, as if he would never come back to me again.

Just at this time I was offered a job in a commercial studio. The pay was two pounds ten shillings a week, more than I had ever earned before. That finally decided me to let Sandro stay away for a time, so I accepted the job, although I had to tell them I would have to leave when Sandro returned, but they said perhaps I could work part time then, so we left it at that.

I was glad to have a regular job. It took my mind off all my miserable feelings. The first day there, I had to walk to work because we had no money in the house. Charles promised he would bring some in time for lunch, but, of course, didn't, and I was too shy of the other girls to borrow any, so I became rather hungry and when it was time to leave I waited to see if he would come to fetch me, but again he failed me, so I had to walk home, getting more and more hungry on the way, and angry, too. When I arrived home I saw Charles through the uncurtained window. He was sitting reading with a tray of tea-things beside him. He looked so comfortable, I became even more angry, and dashed in like a whirlwind and picked up a chair and hit him with it. He did look startled. It was the first time I had done anything like that, and he was disgusted with me. I was ashamed of myself, too, but felt too tired to apologise, so just went to bed and wished I was dead.

But I didn't die. The next morning there was a letter from Peregrine saying he was returning that day and would call round after dinner. I was glad about this, because it was seven weeks since we had seen him and everything had been so miserable. I felt things might be better now he had returned.

When I told Charles he said he was going out that evening. He had arranged to share a model with Francis at his studio, so I would have to entertain him alone. Charles and I were still on bad terms with each other, but it didn't seem to matter any more.

That evening, when I returned from work, I tidied the flat and then myself. Charles had already left the house, so I did not have to cook any supper. I made some coffee and was just laying a tray with the best cups and some chocolate biscuits when Peregrine arrived. He seemed pleased to see me and after a few minutes asked where Charles was. I told him he was out. Then he said he would go and say good night to Sandro, who was very fond of him, so I told him Sandro was out, too, and would be for several months. Then he noticed how thin and awful I was looking and asked what was the matter. He said he was sure something dreadful had happened while he was away, but I changed the subject and told him about my new job, and we sat on the divan and drank coffee and talked about his lecture tour; but I hardly listened. I couldn't help looking at him and thinking how glad I was he was back.

Then he said he insisted on knowing what had happened

while he was away. I didn't like to tell him in case it made him hate me, but he was so insistent that eventually I did tell him, and it did not make him hate me, but he seemed rather shocked, and kept muttering 'If only I'd known' over and over; but I couldn't see that there was anything he could have done if he had known. It was a great relief to get all this misery and guilty feeling off my mind, and no one could have had a more kind and sympathetic listener to load their misery on than I had. I even told him about hitting Charles with the chair, but it didn't seem to matter any more. Charles was miles away.

But not in reality. Very soon he was at home again, with his sketch book under his arm. He was very pleased with the drawings he had done and showed them to Peregrine, but although they were good, he didn't seem interested; he seemed kind of distracted and left almost immediately. Charles said he was 'a surly bugger'.

21

The next day at lunch-time the little man called 'Lonely Pilgrim' who swept out the studio and did odd jobs came and told me in a loud whisper that a Mr Narrow had called for me, so I went to the outer room and there he was. He said he had come to take me out to lunch so that I didn't throw any more chairs at Charles. I was awfully pleased to see him, but hoped I wasn't covered in dirt and paint. I ran away to fetch my coat and saw in the glass I wasn't looking dirty at all; on the contrary, I looked my very best, although I was only wearing a home-made plaid frock that had cost three shillings.

We went to an Italian restaurant in Charlotte Street which was quite near and had a beautiful lunch. I'd quite forgotten how sad I was and chattered away, but he wasn't bored, because he said he would fetch me for lunch almost every day in future to make sure I had at least one good meal a day. He didn't eat much himself, just sat watching me, which I thought rather a waste. I didn't tell Charles about these lunches I had with Peregrine in case he came to the restaurant every day to get a free lunch, too.

I began to think of Peregrine all the time, but this didn't make me unkind to Charles. I was much nicer to him than usual, and always cooked his favourite food for supper, and let him draw me as much as he wished. I kept quite still without grumbling, even when I had masses of work screaming to be done.

One morning before I left for work James 'phoned and asked us to have dinner with him. I said Charles would love to come, but I wanted to have an evening at home to have a great tidy up, and if I had no cooking to do it would be a great opportunity, so it was arranged that Charles should go. When I told Peregrine this at lunch-time, he said, 'Don't go home and do all that stupid tidying. Come and have supper at my studio.' I rather felt it would be deceitful to do this, but, on the other hand, I wanted to very much, so I said I would, but I must leave early so that I could at least make the flat look as if it had been cleaned, and have a smell of polish about. Already I was getting a scheming mind.

When I left work that evening Peregrine was waiting outside to take me to his studio. It was pouring with rain, and his collar was turned up and his hat was turned down, and he looked like a dreadful wet piece of seaweed. He took my arm and we hurried to the nearest bus stop. For the moment I felt almost annoyed with him for waiting in the rain for me like that, and getting so stupid and wet. I felt almost suffocated and wished I had gone home to do my cleaning.

Eventually we arrived at his studio and everything became more cheerful. He had left the gas-fire burning, and the table was laid with a nice clean check cloth and had a bottle of red wine on it, and some daffodils, too.

I felt ashamed of my unkind thoughts as he helped me off with my wet coat. My frock was damp, too, so he made me put on his dressing gown. I was a bit frit of taking off my frock, because all the underclothes I wore was knickers, but the dressing gown was red silk with white spots, and I draped it round me in a fashionable kind of way and felt quite grand except that the sleeves flapped. We cooked the supper over the gas-ring – he didn't have a kitchen, just a large studio and a bathroom. The supper was mixed grill – bacon, mushrooms and the inevitable sausages. It didn't go very well with the wine, but we drank it all the same.

When we had finished eating and drinking, I played the portable gramophone. He had a lot of foreign records – chiefly Spanish. I hadn't heard any before and played them every time I came. After a while I became bored with turning the handle, which fitted badly and kept flying out, so we just talked. I sat on the floor, very near the fire, and he sat in a low chair behind me, and I leant my back against him. It was so comfortable, I couldn't bear the idea of going home and making the flat smell of polish. Then we became silent, and Peregrine came and sat on the floor beside me. Then he began to kiss me; at first I was shy and scared, although I realised now I'd been wanting him to do this for quite a long time. I forgot about being shy and kissed him back. Then I knew I had never loved Charles. I felt I was being carried away in a great, fierce, misty flood.

Some time later, when I realised I had been unfaithful, I didn't feel guilty or sad; I just felt awfully happy I had had this experience, which if I had remained a 'good wife' I would have missed, although, of course, I wouldn't have known what I was missing. I felt quite bewildered. I had had one and a half children, but had been a kind of virgin all the time. I wondered if there were other women like this, but I knew so few women intimately it was difficult to tell.

When I went home I hurriedly put myself to bed. I'd just got in when Charles returned. He stood by the bed talking a little, and asked if I had done my great cleaning, and I found myself answering, 'Oh, no. I didn't feel very well and went straight to bed when I came in.' He said I did look a little feverish. He hoped I wasn't sickening for something. And even then I didn't feel ashamed of myself.

22

There seemed to be unlimited chances of seeing Peregrine at this time. For one thing, Charles went away to stay with his father for a week. Also he joined a sketch club and went there two evenings a week to draw a model in many quick positions, which was very good practice for him. About once a week Peregrine would come to dinner in our flat. He talked about painting to Charles and seemed very friendly, but I almost wished he would never come; it seemed kind of deceitful and lacking in pride.

On the whole, I was very happy at this time. It was beautiful to be in love, and to have someone care so much for me. I didn't feel guilty towards Charles, because it was his own fault in a way. If he hadn't made me destroy my baby this would never have happened. I almost wished I could have a baby by Peregrine to make up for the last one. We had discussed living together, but at the moment it seemed impossible. For one thing, I didn't like to leave Charles while he was earning no money, but the main reason was I was afraid Charles's family would take Sandro away from me if I left him, and put the poor child in a ghastly orphan-age or somewhere dreadful.

I had begun to miss Sandro a lot. At first it had been a relief to know I had not to worry about him while I was out all day, and to know he was having plenty of good food and country air, but I felt depressed in case he was forgetting me. The flat seemed so empty and dull on Sundays. He had been away three months now.

I told Peregrine how much I longed to see Sandro, but where he was staying was such a difficult place to get to by train, and it was so far away I wouldn't have enough money for the ticket in any case, so he said he would try to borrow a car and take me down there. I felt so happy about this. A few days later at lunch he told me he had found someone who would lend him a car the following Sunday. I told Charles and at first he said he didn't want to come in case I made a scene about leaving Sandro behind, but I promised I wouldn't, so he agreed to come. I bought a little Beatrix Potter book for a present. He loved books and did not tear them like most children do.

When Sunday came it was a beautiful spring day, and we started off early. I had written and told the people he was stay-ing with we were coming and would be along before lunch. Peregrine was a good driver, but sat rather forward and crouched over the wheel and talked a lot about driving as if he wasn't really used to it. This seemed rather waddy to me. Then I felt unkind to criticise him after all his kindness. He had even thought to bring a camera so that I could take a few snapshots. We enjoyed the drive so much at first, but gradually we became bored. It was such a long journey and the car was small and old and didn't go very fast and was very bumpy, too. Peregrine kept comparing it to cars he had owned and driven before. The sky clouded, too.

These relations of Charles lived near Evesham and we rather lost our way, but eventually found ourselves surrounded by fruit blossom, so guessed we must be near. We kept crossing the River Avon because we were not sure which side the village was and everyone directed us different ways, but at last we found ourselves outside a charming half-timbered house with gables, and that was Charles's uncle's house.

A thin, sour-faced maid came to the door. She looked all wrong for the house. She asked us into the hall, and then went into a room that sounded like a dining-room, and there was a lot of talk before she came out. Although it was only one o'clock, they had not waited lunch for us, and when the sour maid eventually showed us into the dining-room, they did not seem at all pleased and you could tell they did not like the idea of giving three extra people lunch, although it wasn't wartime or anything, and I had written to warn them. They hardly spoke to us while we tried to swallow our cold beef. It was fortunate the helpings were small, because they kind of stuck in your throat.

When we had finished, Charles's uncle, who was not quite so frigid as his wife, asked us if we would like to see over the 'estate' (the estate consisted of a medium-sized garden and an orchard). I refused, but Peregrine, who had been looking most sinister, agreed to go after we had exchanged glances. I felt we should be as polite as possible even if they were pretty grim.

I asked Charles's aunt, who was a very plain woman with a flat chest and hair on her chin, if I could see Sandro now. I had asked before, but she said he was resting after his lunch, but this time she said she supposed I could. The night nursery was upstairs on the right. I found it easily because the door was open and I saw the nurse lifting him out of a cot. He was still only half awake and when he saw me he started to cry. The nurse said children don't like to see strangers when they first wake up. I told her I wasn't a stranger, but his mother. Then I had another shock. I saw they had cut his hair off unevenly. His skin showed in places. His beautiful red-gold curls had all disappeared. I asked the nurse what had happened. She said 'Madam' liked short hair for boys and had cut it herself. Poor little boy! he was only two and looked like a convict.

When he had woken up properly and been on the pot, he recognised me and climbed on my lap and was most affectionate; but I still felt like there was a great lump in my chest. Charles came in, and after looking at him for a few moments, Sandro remembered him and started to laugh. He had always thought Charles rather funny. The nurse said it was time for his walk and dressed him in his coat and a horrible white tam-o'-shanter. I said, 'He can't wear that; he has never worn a hat in his life. He didn't even wear a bonnet when he was new,' but she said 'Madam' insisted he wore one. Instead of the brown hardy little boy we had sent away, we now had a polite, white-faced child smothered in clothes and lacking hair. The nurse was dressing the little girl cousin. She was quite a pretty little girl with rather a pert, pug-like face. The nurse curled her hair carefully round her fingers. I noticed she didn't have to have a beastly tam-o'-shanter stuck on her head.

We took him out into the garden, although the nurse was worried about him missing his walk. Peregrine was shocked when he saw him, too. I told him I wouldn't use the camera after all, so Sandro showed us the garden. He took us to the orchard, but Charles's aunt hurried after us and said he wasn't allowed in there because of the hens. Apparently he had once taken an egg out of one of the nests and eaten it raw. It seemed a queer thing for him to do. I thought she must have made a mistake, but we didn't go in the orchard. I wondered if she thought I would steal eggs; perhaps that was her real reason for not wanting us to go there.

The afternoon wasn't a great success. Sandro was sweet, but Charles was bored and cross, and Peregrine was very angry and nervy because these people were so rude to us. We decided it would be better if we went home directly after tea. I discovered the children were not allowed to have it with the grown-ups under any circumstances, so I went upstairs and had a nursery tea. Before I went I begged Peregrine to keep his temper, however objectionable they were to him. I felt bad about letting him in for such a dreary day.

I quite enjoyed the nursery tea. The nurse was really rather a sweet old thing; but I was shocked to see Sandro was only allowed watered milk and bread-and-jam without butter, because 'Madam' said he wasn't used to butter and it would make him sick. The little girl said 'Pardon' every time I spoke to her and put her head on one side. I got so tired of repeating myself I left her alone. The nurse said she wasn't really deaf; it was just a habit she had.

After tea I went down to the drawing-room, taking both children with me. The atmosphere was particularly icy. I gathered Charles had mentioned how frightful Sandro's hair was, all tattered and torn like that, and his uncle had said, 'There are enough long-haired people in your family,' and had given him a shilling to get his hair cut. I said I had come down because it was time we went home because we had such a long journey before us. As soon as we started to put on our coats, Sandro began to cry, and say 'Don't go, Mummy, don't go', which made it very hard to leave him. I suddenly remembered there was a bar of chocolate in my pocket which I'd forgotten to give him, so I gave it him in the hope it would stop his sad crying. But the aunt saw and pounced at once. She said: Surely I knew chocolate would give him a temperature, and was almost as bad as poison for a child. So we went away and the last thing we heard was Sandro crying and I cried, too.

Charles and Peregrine exchanged views about the relations, but I just sat in the car feeling numb. It was raining now, and the windscreen wiper made a depressing noise. Suddenly Peregrine stopped the car and said, 'This is where you have a drink, my dear. I think we all need one.' We did and after a double whisky in the small country pub we had stopped at, I felt much better and laughed to think how shocked our late hosts would be to see us now. Charles and Peregrine had a game on an antiquated pin-table, and I looked at the fish in glass cases that were hanging from the walls. There was even a flying fish. Then we had another whisky for the road and went back to the car.

I spent the rest of the journey planning how to get Sandro home again. If I gave up my present job we would have no money to live on at all. Charles had not earned a penny since Christmas. Maybe I could start sitting again, but that was so irregular, and Charles didn't like looking after Sandro while I was out. The only answer to the problem was for Charles to get a job in some studio, so I thought to-morrow, when he had got over this dismal day, I would try to persuade him to look for something. It was a very long time since he had tried to find something. Perhaps jobs were better now the depression was lifting, but in my heart I knew Charles would never take a job in a studio, however attractive it sounded.

23

The next day when I met Peregrine I told him how unhappy I felt about poor Sandro, and he agreed that he would be much better at home than with those dreary people. He said he thought Mr Karam might give Charles a job going round country sales buying Chinese works of art. I couldn't imagine Charles bidding at sales, but it sounded quite interesting, so I asked him to get into touch with Mr Karam about it.

I told Charles about this when I went home, but he didn't seem at all pleased. He said now he was just finding his way as a painter he couldn't waste his time hanging around country sales. He said Sandro was quite all right where he was. He knew at the time it was a great mistake for me to go and see him. If I hadn't been there I wouldn't have known anything was wrong. How could I think he was better off in London when he had such a good country home with every comfort. We talked and talked, but Charles was determined not to have Sandro back if it meant getting a job. His painting came before anything else. In a way, he was quite right. Maybe, the only way to get on is to be ruthless, so I just felt it was useless to continue arguing.

A few days later Mr Karam called. I had rather a sinking feeling in case he mentioned jobs or anything to upset Charles, so I hurried into the kitchen to make coffee, but while we were drinking the coffee he said his friend, Peregrine Narrow, told him Charles was very anxious to get some work and went on to offer him this job of buying Chinese stuff at sales.

Charles looked so angry I felt even more of a sinking feeling. Then he stood up and said, 'Tell Peregrine Narrow to mind his own bloody business,' and after that Mr Karam left, and in his hurry left all his books behind on the table. So I ran after him with them and told him how grateful I was for his kind offer, but he still looked stern and I knew we would never see him again.

Just at this time Charles's mother wrote and suggested paying us a visit. She had never stayed in the new flat. She had made friends with a woman who had a very nice flat in Baker Street, and had stayed with her every time she visited London, but she must have stayed too often, because they had quarrelled and the Baker Street friend was 'that woman' now and drank like a fish and was cruel to her dog and was perfectly dreadful. I suddenly felt I couldn't face having her to stay now. Somehow being in love with Peregrine gave me new courage, so I wrote without telling Charles and I told her it would be most inconvenient to have a guest at the present time. I was out working all day and had no time for visitors. I suggested she stayed in a hotel; if she cared to look around she would find there were plenty in London. She answered with a very fierce letter full of things like 'after all my kindness' and 'ingratitude' and 'that I'd dragged her son down to my own level'. But she didn't come and that was the main thing.

We made it up over the telephone, and on Sunday evening

she came to dinner, bringing a peace offering of a pink silk pleated skirt. I wondered if she would find out if I cut it up and made it into a nighty. After dinner, Peregrine came. I hadn't seen him for two days, so he didn't know Eva would be there. At first she was quite pleased to have an interesting-looking man to talk to, and I left them together while I washed up, but when I came back with the coffee he was just saying Sandro looked far from well, and he didn't think her sister fed him properly, and it was about time Charles found some work and kept his wife and child. I was horrified. Of course, Peregrine was pretty cross about the way Mr Karam's offer had been received, and perhaps he thought he was sticking up for me or something, but I knew it wouldn't do any good, only make a lot of trouble, and it did. Eva drew herself up and said, 'Sophia had no right to marry my son, but as she forced herself on him, she deserves all she gets. She worked for her living before she was married and it won't hurt her to work now. My son is a genius and deserves some consideration.' Peregrine said, 'Who on earth gave you the idea that Charles is a genius?' But before she could reply, I put the coffee down and seized a dirty piece of tangled knitting from under a cushion and pushed it at Eva and asked if she could show me how to knit a polo-neck for a jumper I was knitting for Sandro. She was so angry she was kind of gobbling like a turkey cock, but she loved telling people how to do things properly and took my knitting in her shaking hands and told me it was the most uneven and dirty knitting she had ever come across. While she was telling me how to make polo-necks, Charles came in and Peregrine said he must go. I walked to the door with him and held his hand against my face for a moment to show I wasn't cross, and he was gone.

Eva was telling Charles what a dreadful man he was when I returned. She gave me a reproachful glance and said, 'I'm sure that man is in love with you. He is a snake in the grass. He is the man with a load of mischief.' Charles and I couldn't help laughing, but I had a silly thought that perhaps he was the man with a load of mischief. That was why his back was rather humpy.

Eva returned to the country quite soon, so there was no more trouble of that kind, but things became very strained between Charles and me. Sometimes I thought he must know about Peregrine and I being lovers, but nothing was said, and he usually seemed quite pleased to see him when he visited us, but I was fretting for Sandro all the time and blamed Charles for him being away. I wrote him long letters, but I am sure no one bothered to read them to him. I kept telling Charles I must have him home, and he would go all remote and say he was better where he was, and I would hate him. But when Ann asked when Sandro was returning and said 'Isn't Charles ever going to get a job?' I pretended I wasn't worried and that Charles would be selling his paintings again soon and Sandro was much better where he was. Although I criticised Charles myself, I couldn't bear other people to do so, even Peregrine. It was queer because I didn't love him; in fact, I almost hated him now.

Peregrine and I still met for lunch nearly every day. He would sit gazing at me over the luncheon table and wouldn't eat his lunch at all and made me feel un-romantic eating. Often he met me in the evening and came in the bus with me as far as Abbey Road. Once Charles spent the weekend with James and I stayed the whole weekend with Peregrine. I was afraid the other people in the house would say something to Charles about us both being away or he would 'phone and find me not there; but nothing happened.

That weekend was my highest peak of happiness with Peregrine. The only sad part of it was, when I returned home, I discovered Greedy Min had somehow got out of her bowl and died of thirst. I felt it was a kind of judgment from God.

After that weekend I was not so happy with him. It was not his fault, but I sometimes found him oppressive, kind of stifling, like a thunder-storm, and I would get irritable with him. I was feeling very nervy and depressed because it was five months since Sandro had gone away, and there was still no hope of him coming back. I told Peregrine I would leave Charles and live with him, if he would take Sandro and me to another country where Charles's family would never find us. He said he would make enquiries about jobs abroad. For some reason we picked on Jamaica and I got some books from the Free Library all about life in Jamaica; but that is as far as we got. So it was just a lot of talk and I felt disappointed in Peregrine for taking the matter no further. He seemed to love me so much, but would do nothing about the future. He often said he wished we would have a child, but how could we have one if I was still living with Charles? Now, looking back, I realise he was very romantic and sentimental, but at forty-seven he hadn't the energy or initiative to take on new responsibilities.

24

One evening early in June Ann came round looking important and mysterious. I thought she had either got a lover or a new and better job; but it was neither of these things. She had received a letter from a lawyer to say we had each been left one hundred and fifty pounds – a Great-Aunt Nelly had died and left the little money she had to her nieces. It was years since I'd been in touch with her; in fact, I had forgotten she existed. Now she didn't exist any more. Ann had written her every Christmas and sent a present from the box under her bed. I could just remember her, a little old woman with a face like a fox and an umbrella with a parrot's-head handle.

When Ann told me the great news I was so overcome I put my head in my hands and cried with awful tearing kinds of sobs. She thought I was being a hypocrite, pretending I was mourning Aunt Nelly after neglecting her for all those years; but it was the wonderful relief. Now I could get Sandro home and all our petty debts could be paid. I could buy new shoes instead of always wearing Ann's cast-offs, which were half a size too small for me.

Ann said it would be about a month before we received the actual money, but that didn't seem to matter much. Charles came in just as I was wiping the tears off my face with my skirt. His thin face became rather set when he saw I'd been crying. He thought there was going to be more trouble about Sandro, but when Ann and I together told him the news, he completely changed. He said we must all go to the Café Royal to celebrate. I asked if he had anything to celebrate on. He said, of course he hadn't, but he was sure Ann would lend him two pounds, and to my surprise she did.

We had a lovely evening and Charles and I were happy together for the first time for months. Ann enjoyed herself, too. We had chicken and strawberries and a bottle of red wine – quite cheap, but it tasted nice.

As we were leaving the Café Royal, we saw Peregrine sitting with some men at one of the marble-topped tables. He looked so surprised to see us coming from the part where you dine; I could tell he was a little annoyed. Just coming on him unexpectedly, I couldn't help noticing how old he looked and rather yellow, too. I suddenly thought perhaps it was just as well we hadn't gone to Jamaica; he would have got older and more yellow there, maybe.

The next day I told him my good news, but he didn't seem very enthusiastic, and said one hundred and fifty pounds wasn't much money, and would last a very little time. Then he asked if I was coming to the studio that evening, as it was one of Charles's evenings at the sketch club, but I said I couldn't, because I was so busy. For one thing I was going to paint Sandro's cot and high chair, because he would be home quite soon now, and I must give the paint time to dry. He looked very black and reproachful, and I knew I was unkind, because I could have easily put the painting off one more day.

But it was fortunate that I hadn't arranged to go to the studio because when I arrived home Charles was still there, and had cooked supper all ready for me. He had cooked some fish and mashed potatoes and had decorated the dish with parsley and lemon. It was so nice to come home to. I told him while we were eating that I was planning to give my job up and fetch Sandro home as soon as I received the money, and he said if I couldn't be happy without Sandro I had better have him home. It wouldn't be so bad now I would be home to look after him. So I wrote to Charles's relations that evening, telling them I was leaving my job and would like to have my child home again. Of course, I thanked them very much for looking after him all those months.

A few days later I had a reply. They seemed very annoyed that I wanted Sandro home. I can't think why. They didn't like him except for a kind of foil to their child. They said it was most selfish of me to want him when the only home I had to offer was a pokey little London flat. As a matter of fact, both the rooms in our flat were about three times the size of any room in their house. They also said we led a very 'Bohemian' life, not at all suitable for one of tender years; but if I was so rich I could afford to give up my work, the least I could do would be to pay them something for all the months they had kept Sandro.

I didn't know how to answer this letter, but Charles, to my great surprise, said he would write them a 'stinker'. This seemed to work, because it was eventually arranged that Charles would go to Birmingham and they would meet him there with Sandro in about two weeks' time. After this I began to feel really happy, and Charles and I began to go out in the evenings together again. Often he would meet me from work and we would go to a theatre or film, or just have dinner in a cheap Italian restaurant.

I suddenly realised I was very fond of Charles, not in love with him, but I enjoyed his companionship, and was happy to be with him now there was no reason to feel resentful towards him. He seemed to feel my new fondness for him and fell in love with me all over again. Sometimes when I came home in the evening he would have the supper all ready for me, and if I was tired he would make me go to bed early and read to me aloud. I loved this after all our unhappy times together.

The only thing that was wrong was my conscience. Peregrine was weighing on it terribly heavily. As a matter of fact, I just didn't want him any more. My one wish was never to see him again. I kept trying to tell him, but it was so dreadfully difficult. He must have known my feelings had changed, because I kept making excuses about visiting his studio. Now he would meet me on my way to work and again at lunch and in the evening, too, if Charles wasn't there first. He kept looking at me with hot, reproachful eyes, rather like frying liver, and at lunch-time it was frightful. Now I couldn't eat either, and we sat looking at each other over beastly plates of cooling meat and two vegetables.

After about a week of this I knew I must quickly tell him the truth, so I agreed to go to his studio and he seemed very agreeably surprised, and there he was waiting outside the studio where I worked in the evening. It was very warm, and he was wearing a perfectly beastly blazer – a blue one, at least two sizes too large, and an open-necked shirt, made of awful lock-knit stuff like cheap knickers. I was quite glad to see him wearing such stupid clothes. It made it easier to tell him I didn't love him any more.

When we entered his studio there was a pathetic little supper all ready and flowers on the table as well, so I felt bad again. After we had eaten the pathetic little supper he pulled me over to the divan, and put his hot arm all round me. It was just getting ready to thunder outside and it suddenly became very dark and I felt dreadfully closed in. The room smelt of damp towels and mice, and I couldn't bear it any more. He started to kiss me, but I quickly jumped to my feet, and said, 'Peregrine, there is something dreadful I must say. It's this – I don't love you any more and I don't want to be an adulteress any more either.' I was quite horrified at myself for saying it like that, but it came out so quick.

After that, of course, everything was grim. All the most awful things happened. He put his head in his hands and cried. It made me so shocked and frit, and I longed to escape; but there was rain and thunder going on outside, but, in any case, I thought the least I could do would be to try to cheer him up a little, but he just went on being miserable. I rather had an idea he was enjoying himself in some strange way. He kissed the bottom of my skirt. I said, 'Don't do that. The hem is coming undone already.'

When at last the rain stopped, he let me go home. He came as far as the bus with me. He held my arm very tight and kept saying, 'My God, oh, my God!' although he was an atheist and it wouldn't do any good saying that. When a 28 bus came, it was with difficulty I persuaded him not to accompany me home; but I promised to meet him for lunch the following day, although I couldn't bear the idea.

The next week was perfectly ghastly. I could never make up my mind how much Peregrine was acting or really feeling. I longed to cut him completely out of my life; but I kept remembering all his kindness to me and knew I mustn't be too unkind. All this worried me so much I began to feel quite ill and decided the best thing to do would be to leave the studio and give up my job earlier than I intended, then there wouldn't be those awful lunches, and he would only see me at home and Charles would usually be there.

There was one good thing that happened at this morbid time. Francis put Charles in touch with a man who was about to start a small gallery which was going to exhibit modern English paintings, and it was arranged that as soon as the gallery opened Charles would look after it in the afternoons. The salary would be only one pound a week, but some of Charles's paintings were to be exhibited, so there would be a chance of them selling, and he would be meeting people interested in painting all the time. I was so surprised and pleased at Charles for taking the work, but he seemed almost eager to, but that might have been because he wanted to please me.

25

Charles had gone all the way to Birmingham to fetch Sandro, and I should have been feeling overcome with happiness, but I wasn't. I was feeling scared to death, because I was going to have another baby and it was Peregrine's. It had been inside me for about two months now. At first, in all the excitement of the money and everything, I hadn't noticed anything wrong. I'd forgotten all about periods, but when another month passed I realised what had happened. Why should all these babies pick on me, and always at the most inconvenient times? Charles and I had been so happy lately, and now it was all ruined. I had not told Peregrine yet and I thought perhaps it would be best to tell him to-day, while Charles was away. I was rather hoping I would feel better when I had told him. It wouldn't seem my responsibility so much. My brain had been feeling so numb lately I couldn't think what to do about the future at all.

I went to the public 'phone in the hall and dialled his number. He seemed so pleased to hear my voice. It was over a week since we had last seen each other. He said he would love to come to lunch. I wondered if he would enjoy himself as much as he expected. I went to the shops and bought some eggs for an omelette, and some raspberries. I bought quite a lot so that Charles and Sandro could have some for supper. It was so lovely to have enough money to buy things like that.

When Peregrine arrived he was in very good form. He seemed to think I'd changed my mind about him, 'phoning him like that. He kept saying how pleased he was to see me and how beautiful I was looking. After lunch, when we were drinking our coffee, I told him my news. I was interested to see what his reactions would be. He had always said he very much wished to have a child. His wife had refused to have any – that was one of the things they had quarrelled about. I thought, 'If he really loves me and wants the child, the best thing for us all will be for me to leave Charles and try to start a new life; it can't be much worse than the one I've had up to now.'

I just said, 'I'm going to have a baby and it's yours. It's about two months old now.'

He looked very startled, rather like a frit hen. Then he was thoughtful, but eventually he said quite brightly, 'You could have another operation, couldn't you?'

I said, 'No, I couldn't.'

So he thought again, and suggested I should let Charles think it was his. Just pretend it was born a month premature, and it would appear to be his.

I said, 'Charles simply hates babies, and can't afford to keep his own, so I don't see why he should keep yours.'

I must have sounded rather fierce, because he put on a very sad face, then put his face in his hands, but he cheered quite soon and said, 'Perhaps it will be born dead.'

After this my one idea was to get rid of him now. So I pretended I was going out, and he said he had better get home now. He seemed very glad of an excuse to go, but kissed me before he left and said, 'Let me know if there is anything I can do to help,' and walked away into the sunshine.

When he had gone I lay on the divan and cried till I was sick. I had wild ideas of being a nun, but they wouldn't let you be a nun if you were having a baby. Feeling dreadfully sad and hurt in the night makes you unable to sleep, but in the day-time it is quite the reverse, and soon I became kind of stunned and sleepy. Then I was sick some more, and suddenly went to sleep.

When I awoke I felt quite calm. I looked at the clock and saw that Charles would be home with Sandro in an hour. I went into the bedroom and there was Sandro's cot all aired and ready. Sitting on it was a new teddy-bear that growled. There was nothing else I could do, so I made some tea and washed up the lunch things while I drank it. Then I sat on the steps that led into the garden. I smoked one of Charles's cigarettes, a thing I seldom did, but I thought it might steady me a little while I made my plans for the future.

It was quite plain there would be no help coming from Peregrine, but I had £150, less £5 I'd borrowed from Ann. With this I could run away. Maybe I could start a small business, a book-shop perhaps – but if I took Sandro with me Charles's family would track me down and take him away. On the other hand, I could take the easy course and let Charles think it was his child, born rather early. When it had arrived I could tell him the truth. The only thing about this was the £150 would have been used up by this time and I would have nothing to run away with if he didn't want me after he knew the truth. Then I thought I must tell him I was having a baby as soon as possible, this evening, if he wasn't too tired. If he hated the idea, as he most likely would, I'd tell him he needn't worry, I would go away and take Sandro with me. If I didn't tell him about Peregrine, his family couldn't very well take him away from me.

I found myself hoping I would have a miscarriage. I felt I almost hoped the poor baby would be born dead, as Peregrine wished. Then I was horrified with myself. I thought, 'I've murdered one child, now I'm hoping this one will be born dead. What a wicked woman I've grown into! What has become of me? I used to be quite good once.'

Then Charles and Sandro came home and I made them some tea. But Sandro was so excited he wouldn't eat or drink, but kept running around the flat, opening and shutting doors, and chatting away so fast we couldn't understand what he was saying. In the end he discovered his old toy-cupboard and sat down and pulled everything out. Most of it was junk, but he seemed very pleased to see it again. It was with great difficulty I persuaded him to leave the untidy heap of semi-broken toys. I bathed and put him to bed, and thought how shocked Charles's aunt would be to see him sitting up in bed eating raspberries and cream well covered in sugar.

When we had eaten our supper and Charles was smoking and finishing off his beer, I told him I was going to have this baby, but instead of being overcome with dismay, he was nice about it. I was so surprised tears came in my throat. He said perhaps it would be a girl this time, he would quite enjoy having a daughter, and that he was going to make a great fuss of me this time to make up for all the sad times before, and I felt more wicked and guilty than ever.

26

We decided it would be a good idea to move again. We had had some unhappy times together in our present flat and thought it would be best to start again somewhere. I couldn't help feeling, 'If I'm going to leave Charles in about seven months, it's hardly worth moving now,' but I was getting rather cowardly and kept hoping something would happen, some miracle, and Charles and I wouldn't have to part at all.

So we started flat-hunting. We were looking for something near the Heath or Primrose Hill. I had a great longing to have our own bathroom and not have people always banging on the door. Now if we left our towels and soap in the bathroom, other people would use them, and the bath always had black scum on it. Once when Charles's father came to see us he went to the lavatory and forgot to pull the plug, and an awful old woman ran after him and said, 'You dirty old man, go back and pull that plug at once,' so he did.

With very little trouble we found a most suitable garden flat. It was rather small, but really self-contained. It was all newly decorated in light colours and the sitting-room had a parquet floor, real thick parquet, not just thin stuff laid on top. There was a pretty little bathroom with hot water and every convenience, and a bedroom looking out on to the garden. The kitchen was tiny. It must have been converted from a cupboard. There was just room for a sink, cooker and flap table, which you put down when it wasn't wanted in use. There were plenty of shelves on the walls and you could prepare and cook a whole meal without moving a step.

This flat was in Belsize Square, so we were quite near Primrose Hill. We moved at the end of July, and as soon as we were straight we had a party, so that all our friends would know where we were living. Bumble Blunderbore, whom we hadn't seen for a long time, came. He brought a 'great woman' with him, who really was a great woman. She was quite six feet tall and very beautiful in a totem-pole kind of way, with huge staring eyes, like head-lamps. He was full of how inspiring she was to sculpt. So far he had been unable to finish any of the busts he had started of her, but when he did it would be the best thing he had ever done. All this seemed rather familiar to me. Peregrine was at the party, too. I made rather a point of only having him to the flat when other people were there, too.

A few days after the party we did a thing we had never done together before – we went away for a seaside holiday. We went to Walberswick; James – and, of course, Sandro – came, too. Charles painted most of the time and I lay in the sun and got very brown, and Sandro discovered the sea for the first time. When there was no sun we went for long walks in the woods. In the evening I tried to knit baby-clothes. James was very good at knitting, and did quite a lot for me. People walking past the cottage where we were staying would look quite surprised to see

James in his horn-rimmed glasses, sitting sedately by the door knitting baby's vests.

We were away for a fortnight, and the change did me a lot of good. Often I forgot that the coming baby wasn't Charles's, and I began to feel quite placid. When we returned I bought a radio. Now I was home so much it was a nice thing to have. We didn't have a licence, because I thought only people who had them on hire-purchase had to have licences. By the time I'd discovered my mistake we hadn't a wireless any more. Another wonderful thing we had was our own telephone, and an extra long flex was fixed so that you could even 'phone when you were in the bath. Now Sandro was home we couldn't go out much in the evening, but people often came to see us, and I was quite happy to stay at home and sew or read, and there was the wireless to listen to. Charles sometimes went out by himself, but I didn't feel lonely. I enjoyed sewing clothes for this baby, because I could afford to buy fine and pretty materials. I was determined this baby should have new and lovely things, even if I didn't really want it.

Charles's family were deeply shocked when they heard about us having another baby. Paul wrote and said he would cancel all future help, but as he had only given us twelve pounds in the last three years, we didn't worry. Eva said I had no consideration for Charles. I must control myself and put a stop to all these babies, and in this case, I felt her remarks were quite justified.

The winter came, but we had as much coal as we liked this year. It was lovely to have a fire all day and not go out to work, and to always have enough to eat, clean sheets every week, plenty of hot water – to have all these things at once was almost too good to be true. Sometimes in the afternoon when the house-work and shopping were done, and Sandro having his rest, I would sculpt; but I never got as far as casting anything because I was so afraid of making our beautiful flat dirty. Every day was almost the same, but I liked it like that. In the afternoons Charles went to the gallery and he was happy there. He made a number of new friends, and used to go out with them in the evenings rather often. Sometimes he brought them home for supper and I would cook special dishes. Quite gone were the days when everything I cooked tasted of soap.

As I grew rather fat and full of baby, Peregrine came less and less, so I think he did not like to see me like that, although I didn't look very ugly or bulgy. I didn't stick out behind this time. Then one day he came and told us he had lost his job as art critic. His paper had ceased to take an interest in Art. I felt awfully sorry for him and hoped he had plenty of money saved up, but the next time he came he seemed very depressed and I had a sad feeling that perhaps he was getting short of money, but he didn't say so.

It became very near the time the baby was due. Charles had forgotten all about dates, so I didn't have to pretend and lie about it. I had arranged to go into a nursing-home quite near and was having a room all to myself. It wasn't very expensive, but the actual confinement would just about use the rest of Aunt Nelly's money. Sandro was to stay with some of Charles's new friends while I was away from home. They lived on the outskirts of London and had some children of their own. They were more solid kind of people than Charles's usual friends. I was very glad about this arrangement because I never wanted Sandro to stay with any of my in-laws again.

One morning just before he left home I went into the garden to see if he was up to anything drastic. I found him sitting on the dustbin reading a comic paper; at least, he was looking at one most intently. When he noticed me he jumped off the dustbin and picked up a large pole, and before I could stop him, he said, 'See stars, Mummy,' and gave me a great crack on the head with it. I almost fainted with the shock, and when he saw how much he had hurt me, he was most distressed. When I had recovered a little he pointed, with a dirty, trembling finger, to a picture in his comic paper of a monkey hitting a man on the head and large stars shooting out. That is what he expected to come from my head if he hit it hard enough. That afternoon I took him to Charles's new friends, partly because he was getting rather difficult to manage in my present condition, and also because the doctor came to examine me and said the new baby would come any day now – not that babies often come in the day, they usually choose the night for some unknown reason.

27

A few days after Sandro went away I had a feeling the baby really was coming. I felt very restless and uncomfortable all day and began to wish Charles would come home long before he was due. He didn't like me to 'phone the gallery, but I wished very much to talk to someone. There seemed to be a great loneliness about the flat, so I 'phoned Peregrine, but when I got through a strange man answered and said Mr Narrow had left the studio some time ago, and he gave me his new number. I wrote it down, but did not telephone him. I felt so surprised at him not telling us he had moved. We had seen him only three days ago and he had not mentioned it. I thought possibly he had moved to a cheaper room or flat and was ashamed for us to know.

After all, I did not tell Charles that I'd a feeling the baby was coming that night, because he never seemed to believe babies were coming until they were practically there, and now he was home, I'd quite recovered, and ate a large supper and still felt quite well. However, during the night rather a pain came in my tummy, so I sat up in bed and wondered if I should wake Charles. Then I saw my mother's ghost sitting in the rocking-chair, and it was rocking in quite a normal way, so I did wake Charles and said, 'Look! there is my mother's ghost! She must have come to tell me it's time to go to the nursing-home. I do feel a bit queer.' Then Charles saw her, too, but he didn't like her much. He jumped out of bed and put the light on, and she wasn't in the chair any more, but it still rocked. We got dressed because I was quite sure she wanted me to go to the nursing-home, but seeing a ghost had made Charles a bit grumpy. Afterwards he told me he was so scared he kept the light on all night every night until I returned.

He went out and got a taxi and when I went to get inside it there was a kind of tramp sitting in front by the driver, and when we arrived at the nursing-home, the taxi-driver and the tramp came in, too, and sat on a bench in the hall. I was taken into a ground-floor room and examined by the matron, and she said although I hadn't had much pain the baby was well on the way. So Charles went into the hall and waited with the tramp and taxi-driver, but when the doctor came he shooed them away.

Although I had a more difficult confinement this time, it was so wonderful to lie in bed and not be chivvied about all the time and it wasn't embarrassing at all. The baby took a long time coming and when it did come I was so tired I didn't care what kind it was or if it was alive or dead; but after I'd been asleep I felt more interested, but didn't like to ask to see it in case it was like Peregrine, or in case there was some mark on it to let people know it wasn't my husband's child. Then Charles came to see me and told me it was a very pretty girl. I was relieved to hear that and the nurse brought her out of her cot and gave her to me. I was so surprised to see such a beautiful baby. She had long black hair and round pink cheeks with dimples in. She wasn't red at all, and I couldn't help loving her.

I stayed in the nursing-home for two weeks. Charles came to see me nearly every day. He seemed to quite like this baby and made some drawings of her asleep. I could not bring myself to tell him he was not the father until we returned home. I felt dreadfully hurt that Peregrine hadn't been to see me. He knew about the baby. Charles said he had met him the day after the baby arrived.

When I came home I found Charles had had a charwoman to clean the flat and everything was looking delightful. We had tea and I gave the baby its six o'clock feed. It was a hungry baby, not delicate like Sandro had been. When I put her to bed, Charles became restless and after fidgeting about for a time and saying 'Well' rather often, he suddenly said, 'I've just remembered I have to meet a man for dinner. When I made the arrangement I didn't realise it was the day you were coming home. It's too late to put him off now, so do you mind dreadfully if I go?' 'Of course,' I said, 'do go,' so he hurried off, like a child snatching some extra play. The next evening he came home straight from the gallery, but after that he often did not come till nine or ten, and sometimes it was one o'clock. He seemed to have made even more new friends since I'd been in the nursing-home. He brought some of them home, but they seemed very bored and restless kind of people, and sometimes Charles would say some-one was coming for dinner, and I would prepare a beautiful meal and they wouldn't turn up, and the next time they met Charles they would say that at the last moment they couldn't face the long, complicated journey to Belsize Park, and Charles would say if only we had a flat at Bloomsbury or Soho we wouldn't be so cut off. I loved our present flat; already all the bulbs I'd put in the garden were showing. There would be no gardens in Soho. I'd almost forgotten I was leaving Charles, so it was hardly my concern if he moved to Soho or anywhere else.

Sandro was most interested in the new baby. He used to ask if she was a princess. He was rather jealous of Charles drawing her, but when he painted her he stood sadly by and eventually said, 'I tell you what's wrong with this house, no one paints me.' Charles was very touched by this and made a very good painting of him. We called the baby Frances Charlotte, but quite soon she was called Fanny.

Eva came to see her and said, 'That baby is not at all like Charles. None of my babies looked like that.' So I said, 'I'm sorry you are disappointed in the baby. As a matter of fact, she resembles my family.' Eva had never seen any of my family except me, so I felt quite safe saying that. When I'd been home ten days Peregrine called. I'd felt very wretched about him not coming to see his beautiful daughter, but the last few days I'd almost forgotten all about him. Now when he came I remembered how I had planned to be beastly to him when he did come, so I put on a horrible face and grim manner, but he was so contrite and humble I forgave him. He said he hadn't come before because he thought it might upset me to see him. I thought this rather a feeble excuse, but he got away with it because he was so deeply impressed by Fanny's beauty. He stayed to tea and I asked him why he hadn't told us about his move. He looked rather embarrassed, then said he was staying with relations, and couldn't think why he had not told us about it at the time. So I thought, 'Poor man! he is so hard up he has to live with his relations!'

The next day he came again, and he brought a brush and

comb in a pretty little box for Fanny, and a red truck full of bricks for Sandro. After that he came nearly every afternoon. He was completely fascinated by Fanny. He often came in a car he had borrowed from his relations, and sometimes, as the weather became warmer, took us drives into the country, which I simply loved.

When Fanny was six weeks old I cashed a cheque for five pounds, and that was the end of my banking account. I had no more money. The five pounds lasted for two more weeks' house-keeping. Then I had to ask Charles for money. He only earned one pound a week and spent much more than that in the evenings with his new friends. I think he must have started to borrow money, because he sometimes gave me a pound, but I could only pay for a few days' food with this, and the rest of the week there was nothing. I told Peregrine all my money had gone, but he said 'What a pity!' and nothing else. Perhaps he hadn't got any himself. I began to feel frightened and depressed, and thought, 'This is my punishment for being an adulteress.' Then I remembered I was even poorer before I was one, so per-haps it was a punishment for something I had forgotten.

28

Charles was out more and more in the evening, and it was dull and lonely when the children had gone to bed and there wasn't any supper to eat to pass the time. Peregrine usually stayed till about seven. He liked to watch me putting Fanny to bed and to see her being fed. One day I asked Charles if I could meet him in the evening and go out, too. He said, 'Of course, darling,' but I could see he didn't want me, so I didn't go. In any case I would have had to hurry home at ten to feed Fanny. I began to feel rather dull and unwanted and wondered if having two children had made me grow ugly and unattractive. I looked in the glass for a long time, but seemed to look the same as usual; perhaps I was so used to my face I could not see the difference. I asked Peregrine if I had changed for the worse, and he told me I was still beautiful and that he still loved me as well. I was awfully grateful to know someone did.

Then he told me he had no real work and only had the very little money he earned lecturing. He thought it was only a matter of time till he got another post on a newspaper, and when he did he hoped I would go and live with him and bring the children. I said I would think it over, and when he had gone, I did. I lay in the bath – always my best thinking-place – and thought very carefully. I had been feeling very fond of Peregrine lately. It was partly to do with Fanny and partly because he had been kind when I was lonely. Charles did not seem to want me any more, so perhaps it would be a relief to him if I told him I was leaving him and taking the children, too. Maybe I could even do it without telling him about Fanny. I had been a coward about this right from the first. I was still fond of Charles. Recently we had drifted very far apart. If I had not felt so guilty I would have tried to make him interested in me again; as it was, I couldn't very well object to him leaving me alone in the evenings, or complain about all the money he was spending when we hadn't even enough for food. I felt my treatment was just about what I deserved. So, thinking in the bath, I came to the conclusion it would be best for us to go to Peregrine.

The next day a man came and cut the gas off. The Gas Company had been threatening to do this for a long time. Later on the light was cut off, then the telephone, but we could still get calls in. I missed the gas dreadfully. There was nothing to cook with and the Ascot wouldn't make any more hot water, so I was unable to wash the children's clothes. I tried washing the nappies in cold, but it wasn't a success. Another awful thing, we couldn't have baths.

Now everything was so uncomfortable Charles hardly came home at all. He did buy a hundredweight of coal and I tried cooking on the open fire, but it was a messy business and the coal didn't last long. In the afternoon I used to take the children on Primrose Hill and fill the pram with sticks, which were very useful to boil kettles on. When Peregrine came to see me he was very grieved to see the sad state we were in. He said he wished he could help but was almost penniless himself; but one evening he brought a cold chicken and some salad with him and we had a picnic. I saved quite a lot for Sandro to have the next day. I told Peregrine if he really wanted us I would gladly go to him, but we couldn't wait too long or we might starve to death.

Ann came to see me and she said she would like some tea. I tried to put her off, but she went on wanting it, so I had to light some sticks in the grate to boil the kettle. She thought I was batty, so I had to explain about the gas. She asked why I didn't get an electric ring and I had to say the light had gone, too. She was awfully shocked and said I must be a great spendthrift to have got through all Aunt Nelly's money within a year. She still had over a hundred left. I told her it had all gone on food and rent and the expense of Fanny's birth – £150 wasn't very much for a family of three, and lately four, to live on. She spent about twice that amount on herself a year. Then I started to cry. I was always doing it lately. She looked rather distressed and went without waiting for the tea. When she had gone I saw she had left a pound on the tea-tray. I felt ashamed to take it, but it would pay the milkman for several weeks, so I kept it. I didn't tell Charles. After she had gone I still felt sad. I couldn't help remembering how full of hope and happiness I had been when Ann first told me about Aunt Nelly's money, and now things were much, much worse than before. That evening when Peregrine came I became his mistress again. There seemed no point in being good or bad; everything was so dreadful in any case.

29

After that things got rapidly worse and to make things even more dreary than ever I began to feel ill. It started by my hardly ever going to sleep at night, and in the daytime I would suddenly start to shiver until my teeth chattered, and sometimes I fainted. One good thing, I never felt hungry now. I couldn't feed Fanny any more, but the milkman was kind and let me have milk although we owed him quite a lot. I told Peregrine how difficult it was to buy enough milk for Fanny, but although he seemed to love her, he never offered to pay the milk bill and I couldn't bring myself to ask him. In the night when I couldn't sleep I used to feel resentful about this, but I tried not to think of it, because he was the only person I had to rely on now, and if I lost faith in him there was nobody to turn to. I hardly saw Charles now. Often he didn't come home for several days.

One morning the people who had had Sandro to stay when I was in the nursing-home telephoned to say they had heard I wasn't very well and wondered if I would like to send Sandro to them for a week or two. I was pleased about this, because I was so worried about his food. He had been living on eggs and tinned soup supplied by the kind milkman. I washed and ironed his clothes as well as I could under the circumstances, but they looked rather messy. I did hope they wouldn't think I was a dirty mother.

Charles took him there because it was difficult for me to get about with Fanny. To my surprise, he came back early that evening. I thought it was kind of him because he must have known I was missing Sandro. I managed to boil some eggs and even make coffee on the flame provided by the sticks, and felt more cheerful than I had lately. I was pleased about Charles coming home like that. He didn't talk much. He seemed to be thinking deeply. Then he said, 'We can't go on like this. Could you go and stay with your brother?'

I was rather surprised and told him my brother had ignored me since the visit I paid when Sandro was a baby and I'd so overstayed my welcome. I was quite sure he wouldn't have me to stay again. In any case, we hadn't got enough money to pay my fare anywhere and no one would want me with two children. He said he could find me my travelling expenses if I would find somewhere to go. I said, 'There just isn't anywhere I can go to, except your relations, and I won't stay with them.' He said, 'I wasn't suggesting that you should stay with them; there must be somewhere else.'

He looked so worried and kept catching his breath as if he was going to speak, but nothing came. We both sat in separate huddles on the divan. It was nearly dark, and I felt frit of what he would say next. For some time we were quite silent. Then he said, 'I'm going to be honest with you. I expect you have a pretty good idea of what I'm going to say, and have realised I don't love you any more. I am very fond of you, but I loathe this domestic

143

life. The children are quite beautiful, but they don't mean a thing to me. I don't feel like a father and have never wanted to be one. I may be inhuman and selfish, but I must be, life is so short, and the young part of our lives is going so quickly. I must be free to enjoy it and not be weighted down by all these responsibilities.'

I said, 'Did you often go to *Peter Pan* when you were a child?'

'You are crazy! What on earth has that to do with it?'

I didn't answer, but what I meant was, Charles seemed to have a kind of Peter Pan complex, that he had no responsibilities, and I was a waddy sentimental Wendy, full of mother-complexes, and middle-class comforts, and woolly vests and things, but I wasn't like that at all. I couldn't explain, though, so I said, 'All right, Charles. I see how you feel. I'm not the waddy, suffocating kind of woman you think me, and, of course, we will part. I'll make my plans. Already there are some quite good ones in my head, so don't worry.'

Charles suddenly kissed the top of my head. 'I don't really think you are suffocating. You're sweet, and I feel guilty about you and the children. Sometimes it's almost made me hate you. I've been unfaithful to you lately, but I don't love any woman. I never will again. I must be free.'

He went to the window and stood with his back to me, looking at the daffodils. When he turned round, it almost seemed as if he had tears in his eyes, and we looked at each other and he was gone and I was alone in the flat with Fanny.

I longed to go to bed although it was still quite early. I felt all shivery and my throat was sore, but I must be gone before Charles returned. I went to the telephone to get into touch with Peregrine, but before I lifted the receiver I remembered it was cut off. So I went to the bedroom. There was Fanny, looking so beautiful and peaceful asleep, it seemed a pity to disturb her. I collected a few clothes and toilet utensils and put them in a case, and took a large fluffy shawl which I carefully wrapped round Fanny, and I picked her up very gently so that she did not waken, and we left the flat for ever.

Peregrine was now living in Chelsea, so I walked to Swiss Cottage station to get a bus, a 31. It was difficult carrying a baby and a case at the same time, but a bus came quite soon. Unfortunately, I had only twopence in my bag and couldn't have a very long ride. We got out at a very dreary place called Chippenham. It was getting late, and some men were singing in a depressing, drunken way. There was an overwhelming smell of fried fish. I could see through uncurtained windows rooms that were stiff with iron bedsteads and dirty bedding. Children were still playing on the doorsteps. Some had made sad-looking swings by tying string across the railings. I felt afraid in case my children ever had to live a life like that, and was glad when we reached Notting Hill Gate.

I sat on the steps of the station with Fanny on my knees for a time. I felt so tired and my throat was sore; it made me keep swallowing. I went on and tried to hurry, because Peregrine's relations would think it queer if I arrived in the middle of the night. I hoped he had told them about me. My arms became so tired. I tied Fanny round me in the shawl, but I didn't tie it properly, and it came undone. I only succeeded in catching her just before she reached the pavement. I was so overcome by horror in case she had been killed, I leant against the wall shivering and holding her so close to me she awoke and began to cry. When I reached the Fulham Road I discovered I'd lost the case.

I must have dropped it when the shawl came undone. I couldn't bring myself to retrace my steps all that distance, so went on. I felt insecure without it, and no money in my bag, awfully like a tramp.

At last we came to King's Road and were nearly there. Peregrine lived in a road opposite the Town Hall, I remembered him saying. The streets were so empty now I felt it must be quite twelve o'clock. I hoped everyone in Peregrine's house hadn't gone to bed. I was sure of a welcome from him, but felt pretty scared about his relations. If they didn't know about me it would make such a lot of explaining in the middle of the night. I thought the best thing in the world would be to get into a large bed with clean linen sheets and sleep for ever.

I saw the Town Hall and there was Felix Street. In the lamp-light the houses looked so pretty. They all had brightly painted doors of unusual colours. Number Seven had a mauve door. I'd never seen one before, and admired it for a moment, then lifted the beautifully polished knocker and gave a small knock. I became braver and gave a large knock that echoed down the still street. There was the noise of a door shutting and the click of high heels and the door opened. The tall woman who opened the door seemed vaguely familiar. I tried to remember where I'd seen her before.

I said, 'I'm sorry to be so late, but could I see Mr Peregrine Narrow?'

The woman looked surprised. She had a large, flabby, white face and looked rather like a determined oyster. She pulled her purple house-coat to make it meet in front and said, 'Mr Narrow has gone to bed. If you are a model and wish to see him you had better call in the morning. No! on second thoughts, there is no

146

reason for you to call. He is not using models just now. Good night.'

She began to close the door, and I cried out, 'Please don't shut me out. Tell Mr Narrow it's Sophia. Tell him I've come.'

The woman's heavy jaw dropped. She looked kind of scared and began to close the door, but I slipped in before she quite shut it. I heard Peregrine shouting something, and he suddenly appeared wearing a dressing gown, the same one I'd worn when my clothes had got all wet. In his hand he held a tooth-brush all neatly spread with tooth-paste. He said, 'Good God, Sophia! what are you doing here?'

I went up to him and took his hand and said, 'Do be pleased to see me, Peregrine. I've come earlier than we expected. Do tell this woman about me. Haven't you told her anything about me at all?'

She didn't seem to like being called a woman, because she said, 'My dear Perry, please tell this little model or whatever she is to leave the house at once,' and to my amazement, he said, 'Yes, of course, dear. Sophia, go home like a sensible girl. I'll come and see you in the morning, really I will. But please go. You don't realise how late it is or what a disturbance you are making.'

It was like a nightmare and he was looking so scared – the tooth-brush in his hand was all shaking. I suddenly realised this horrible old woman was his wife, so I said, 'Peregrine, is this hideous old person your wife? I suppose you have gone back to her because she is keeping you.' I was so angry and hurt I would have said a lot more, but the 'hideous old person' took me firmly by the shoulders and ordered Peregrine to open the door, which he did without looking at me, and I was put outside rather quickly.

I stood by the mauve front door for a minute or two. I had ideas of kicking it down and breaking the windows, but most of all, I wanted to smash that beastly woman's face to a pulp. I guessed Peregrine was having a pretty grim time inside, and was glad. After the anger passed I felt so tired and afraid. There was nowhere to go at all, but I walked away. After a time I found myself by the river. I hadn't the energy or will-power to jump in. I was burning and freezing cold at the same time, and was glad of the warmth that came from Fanny.

For a long time I must have wandered about without knowing where I was going, but eventually found myself in Fleet Street. In a dark side-turning, I discovered quite an inviting doorstep and thought I'd better sit there till morning and I could think better. I was shivering so much my teeth made awful clicking noises and the pain in my throat was terribly fierce, so I sat there to wait till the morning came.

30

When the morning came I didn't know much about it. I could
hear Fanny crying. She seemed to be a long way away. I knew
she was crying because she was hungry – it was such a long time
since she had had a meal. I kept dreaming I was feeding her,
then I would wake up with a start and she was still crying. It hurt
when I opened my eyes. Once I saw several people looking at
me. They came near and tried to see Fanny, but I told them to
go away, and went to sleep again. Then someone was shouting
loud and touching me. It was a policeman, so I guessed they
were going to take me to prison for using their doorstep. I tried
to stand up so that I could run away, but I couldn't. Then I discovered they'd taken Fanny away, so I began to cry. The
policeman kept asking me questions, but I couldn't answer. All
I could say was 'Fanny, Fanny'. So he wrote that down. After a
time I seemed to go to sleep again.

The next thing that happened was, I found myself in a police
station. They were very kind and tried to give me a hot drink,
but I was too sleepy to drink it. A doctor examined me. I asked
for Fanny, but she was gone. Tears kept running down my face

all the time, and I felt very strange. I tried to tell them to feed Fanny, but the words wouldn't come properly. I remember being moved about rather a lot. Then a wonderful feeling of comfort came – I was in bed at last, but my heart was beating so loud it seemed to be in my head. There were screens round the bed; all the same, I could tell it was a hospital.

Days must have passed. Once they showed me Fanny. They said it was Fanny, but she didn't look the same. Once there was Charles standing by my bed. He was dressed all in white and his face looked kind; but my throat hurt so much I couldn't talk.

One morning they took the screen away, and I was in a large ward with fourteen beds in it. They said I was getting better and gave me some soup in a feeding-cup. I listened to the other women talking and after a day or two discovered we had all got scarlet fever. I asked if I could see Fanny and they said I could when I was stronger. She had had fever, too. The nurses were so good and kind, quite different from the ones in the maternity hospital. It was so peaceful. I felt too tired to think about the past or future, and slept most of the time. Sunday was visiting-day. I rather dreaded it because I didn't want to be reminded of the existence of a world outside. At three o'clock the visitors all trooped in, wearing white coats and hoods to keep the germs off them. One Sunday when I was recovering, Charles came. He was shy to be dressed in those white robes and had them all open in front and did not wear the hood at all. He seemed to be shy of me, too. I asked him how Sandro was and he said he was very well and happy, and the friends he was staying with were willing to keep him till I left the hospital.

Then I asked him if he had seen Fanny and he replied that

he'd seen her once. He looked kind of queer when he said that, and I felt frightened and had a deep, sinking feeling.

'Tell me, Charles, is she dead?' I asked.

And he answered, 'Yes, she died three days after you came here. They showed her to you just before she died.'

I felt overcome with sadness. Somehow I'd known she was dead all the time. I'd hardly dared to ask after her in case they told me the truth, and now I knew it and there was no escape. If I hadn't exposed her to a night on a doorstep she might have had the strength to recover. Poor, beautiful little Fanny! her life had been wasted because of stupidity and poverty. I felt everything was hopeless and dreaded the thought of leaving the hospital and facing the grim and beastly life that was waiting for me. I told Charles to go, and pulled the sheet over my face and prayed to die.

God must have heard, because two days later I had a relapse and was put in a kind of cage, which they put in my bed and filled with electric light bulbs all burning away. It was so hot. I lay all burning and waiting to die. I took no notice of the kind nurse, or Charles when he came. I couldn't bear to see him, because he belonged to the frightening life I couldn't face any more. One day I vaguely knew he was there all day, and wished he would go away. People kept coming round all the time. It began to seem as if I was coming out of myself, as if I was floating above my body. It was quite a nice feeling when I got used to it. Then I thought, 'Now I'm getting dead and I'll have to meet God and see Him every day for ever, ever more.' I could imagine Him a slightly dense, angry old man, with woolly hair, wearing a striped blanket, and I seemed to remember reading in the Bible He had feet made of brass, and I thought of heaven as a comfortless kind of place, where you had no bed or fire, no sun, books, or food; you'd never see the leaves blowing about on the trees, everything would be still, and Moses would be there, and those terrifying brass feet always. I started to say, 'Please, God, don't let me go to heaven. Let me just lie in my grave and have some peace,' but I realised He wouldn't approve of that. I'd got to be punished for all my sins, so I said, 'Please, God, let me go on living and have my punishments now, and when they are over let me have a peaceful grave and no heaven.'

God must have heard that, too, and I was sorry I had thought Him dense. I began to recover, and every day I was better than the one before. Soon I would have to leave the hospital, but didn't know where to go and I didn't care either. Then my brother wrote. He had heard how ill I'd been from Ann, and he said I could stay with him and bring Sandro, too, if I liked. It was a relief to have somewhere to go to. He also sent five pounds, for which I was very grateful. The future seemed to be arranging itself without any trouble on my part, as if it knew how tired I was.

The last day in hospital all my things had to be baked and my hair washed so that I took no germs away. I was sorry to leave. Charles came to fetch me. He had brought some of my clothes in a suitcase. He said the rest of my things were at Ann's flat. He had given up the flat at Belsize Square and sold the furniture. He paused after he said this as if he expected me to bemoan the loss of my treasures, but I didn't care hardly at all. Everything seemed so remote now – the Staffordshire china, and round oak table, and sea-green furniture – all seemed so far away. Outside in a taxi Sandro was waiting engrossed in a comic paper. He seemed delighted to see me and was looking so well, and wearing all new clothes the people he had been staying with must have bought him. Charles took us to Paddington and put us on the Leamington train. He seemed very relieved to get us there and shut the carriage door firmly and talked brightly about the lovely time I would have, living with my brother in the country. He seemed to take it for granted that we were going to stay there permanently. I think that was why he sold the furniture in such a hurry, to make sure that we couldn't return.

31

My brother and his wife agreed it was hopeless for me to return
to Charles, or expect any help from him. They said I must get
a post as lady cook-housekeeper somewhere in the country
where I could have Sandro with me. I hated the idea of being a
cook-housekeeper. They advertised in the *Telegraph* and *Times*,
and quite a lot of replies came. They showed them to me, but I
hadn't the heart to look at them, so my sister-in-law very kindly
answered the most suitable letters. She ignored the ones from
widowers who required photographs, and lonely men whose
wives had left them. After I'd been there three weeks they told
me they had arranged for me to go as cook to a gentleman
farmer called Redhead, who lived in Bedfordshire. His wife was
an invalid and there were two grown-up daughters.

Joyce, my sister-in-law, helped me to pack my clothes. I only
had summer ones and they were long and arty. She said I had
better not wear them unless it was terribly hot, and she bought
me a tweed coat and a tweed skirt (they were brown) and two
woollen jumpers and a pair of brown lace-up shoes and two spotted overalls – the overalls were the nicest things she bought.

Sandro had quite a lot of new clothes Charles's friends had given him.

When the day came for us to leave I think they were quite sorry to lose Sandro, who had behaved beautifully all through the visit. They must have found me very heavy going, because at this time I'd become completely dull and lifeless. The only thing that I was in the least interested in was Sandro, and I daren't love him much in case he died or disappeared.

I dreaded going to the farm, but when I arrived there it was very much better than I expected. Things one dreads usually are: it's only the things we look forward to that go all wrong. Mr Redhead was a huge, rather pompous man, with a long tweed jacket. He looked rather like Mr Todd. The daughters were large, too, with very fair hair and rosy cheeks. They were called May and Rose and looked just like those names.

It was two days before I was introduced to the mother. She was quite different from the rest of the family. May took me to her bedroom, which she never left. It was in a frightful state of untidiness and dirt, and she sat in her four-poster bed looking like a princess. She was tiny and fair and perfectly beautiful. There was a white cockatoo perched on the end of the bed and its droppings were everywhere, and there were great holes all over the floor that it had made with its beak, and there were holes in the bed-clothes, too. They were made by small African mice with long legs that lived in a cage by the bed. She would let them loose in her bed and forget about them, and they would take bits of the blankets to make their nests with. At first she thought I was a guest come to stay until May explained I was the new cook, and she said, 'How nice to have such a charming cook. I hope you will often come and see me, dear, and perhaps you will sometimes take my poor Poodle for a walk. He is getting a very strange shape from lack of exercise.' On a chair was a great mat of brown fur, which I'd mistaken for an old fur coat. I looked around the room for more animals, but there were only some love-birds in a cage by the window.

Mrs Redhead took no interest in the house, which was run by her daughter May, who took the housekeeping very seriously. It was a large, uncomfortable place, full of Victorian furniture. The carpets had great holes in them and no one seemed to care. The only comfortable chairs were always filled with smelly, but nice, spaniels. There was never any hot water and there were only lamps and candles, but the family loved their home and after a time I became fond of it, too.

I stayed at the farm for three years. I cooked large joints on hot Sunday mornings when I longed to be out in the sun; I preserved fruit and made jam and felt like a squirrel in the autumn when I looked at my full cupboards; I cooked pheasants and soufflés for dinner-parties that I didn't attend, and made cakes for tea-parties for guests that I saw through the kitchen window; I pressed Rose's evening frocks when she went to dances, and answered the telephone to make appointments for the girls to go riding with their friends.

All the days were the same except for one black period when Mrs Redhead died. I used to spend most of my spare time in her room, and she would tell me about her youth and get me to take her old ball frocks out of the huge cupboard, and give me accounts of all that had happened where she wore them. She also had a surprising mania for detective stories. They kept coming from Harrod's in large parcels. As soon as I finished reading one batch another would arrive – she liked me to read to her out loud, and I pretended to like them, too. Sandro would sit on a little stool and listen and enjoyed them almost as much as she did. They would discuss them together when I finished reading. She was very fond of Sandro and paid for him to attend a rather expensive day-school near. I missed her dreadfully when she died.

The only other event of importance during those three years was that I received a letter from Charles asking me to divorce him. This letter upset and frightened me at first, but eventually I showed it to Mr Redhead, who had heard some of my story from my sister-in-law. He took me to his family lawyer, who arranged for me to have a Poor Person's divorce, and except for the fact that I had to appear in court to give evidence, it wasn't too alarming. As far as I know, Charles hasn't married again.

After Mrs Redhead died everything went on the same as before. There wasn't quite so much work perhaps. I had the old poodle and cockatoo in the kitchen and Rose hung the love-birds in her bedroom. No one wanted the African mice much so Sandro had them in the end, but I didn't let them make holes in the blankets. The family paid his school fees now. It was a help to have him out of the way during the busy part of the day, because I couldn't keep an eye on him all the time and Mr Redhead got annoyed if he went about the farm by himself. He was awfully fussy and always thought Sandro was planning to leave gates open or play on the ricks or let the bull out. Actually, he never attempted to do any of these things. He did once stir the bees up with a stick and got badly stung, but no other harm was done. Still, it was good of him to pay for him to go to school.

I had a charming bedroom in an older part of the house.

Sandro had a small one leading out of mine. I painted the furniture blue and distempered the walls and it became quite homelike. There were large casement windows. Often in the afternoon I would sit on the window-sill and look out on the fields and woods, and, in the distance, the hills; but if I stayed there long I would find myself thinking too much. I would worry about how the years were flying away and all my youth was going. I was twenty-four when I first came to the Redheads. Now I'd become twenty-seven. I hadn't a single friend; it was years since I had even been out to tea, or had seen a play or film. Except for Sandro there was nothing to live for. The country was beautiful and peaceful, but I found myself longing for London. I would have given anything to walk down a typical London street made of rather dirty yellow bricks, the houses tall and semi-detached, with a flight of steps going up to the front door, and iron railings with rather straggly privet hedges encaged behind, and every now and then a cat asleep on a window-sill. I could imagine a man passing down the street disturbing the giant pigeons by shouting out the name of an evening paper, and a smell of toast in the air, and at the poorer end of the street, small boys would be making a frightful din on their roller skates. I longed to be queen of my own home with all my treasures around me. I would look out of the window at all the beauty, but it wasn't what I wanted.

32

There were day-old chicks cheeping away round the boiler; the cat had kittens on the mangle, and it was spring again.

Rose became engaged to a young man she had met quite recently at a dance and they were going to be married almost immediately, so there was great excitement in the house. Parcels of clothes kept coming and they were all piled up on the spare-room bed. Some were lying half out of their boxes and tissue-paper was scattered everywhere. Then wedding presents started to arrive and were massed about in the drawing-room. The old grand piano was quite weighed down by toast-racks. Eventually one leg broke under the pressure of toast-racks, but perhaps it wasn't only that that caused the leg to fall off, because it was discovered to have worms and had become quite hollow. There were other presents, too, rather dim etchings and rose bowls and some quite nice coffee- and tea-sets, and quite a lot of grand silver objects. May urged Rose to write and acknowledge all these gifts, but she used to hide in her bedroom and eat bars of chocolate and read *Holiday House*, which made her cry, so May had to write all the 'thank-you' letters eventually.

Rose was completely lazy, and if I asked her to bring some vegetables from the kitchen-garden, she would say, 'Yes, darling Mrs F.! I will bring a whole basketful; just tell me what you want.' And she would pick up a large shallow basket and perch a green, wide-brimmed hat on her head and disappear down the garden. Sometimes she didn't appear again; other times she would turn up after about an hour with a few pea-pods and a carrot in the basket, and laughing, would say that was all the vegetables there were in the garden.

Rose was going to Cairo when she married. Her husband, who was in the Air Force, was being sent there. Sometimes he would fly low over the house and make a dreadful din, and when we ran outside to see what was happening, he would drop a message tied to a stone for Rose. People in the village complained a lot about this, and eventually Mr Redhead put a stop to it because the noise made one of the cows slip a calf before her time.

The preparations for the wedding made a lot of work. The house was spring-cleaned. All the mouldy old carpets were taken up and we beat them on the lawn with beaters made of cane, but still they looked awful. Rose got the idea of sweeping the drawing-room chimney by dropping a goose down it. She said the people in the village often did it, but it made a frightful mess when it ran squawking round the room, flapping its sooty wings. We had to distemper the walls after that. We took down all the bed-hangings and washed them, but some were so rotten they fell to pieces in the wash-tub. We found a dead bat and mouse in Mr Redhead's room. They must have been there ages, but they didn't smell much, because they had become all dried. Although Mr Redhead was glad Rose was getting married, he became rather grumpy about all the upheaval. He used to get cross with Sandro if he even climbed a tree, but, fortunately, the holidays were not due till after the wedding, so he was at school most of the day.

There was not enough time to get all the clothes together for a white wedding, so Rose was wearing a soft blue two-piece suit trimmed with fur. I went into the spare room and looked at it every day. I would have so loved to have been married in something like that, but all I had was a horrid skirt that kept coming unwrapped. May was to be the only bridesmaid and it was with great difficulty she was persuaded to buy a new frock. She was quite uninterested in clothes.

When the wedding-day actually came I got up very early to prepare the food. There was to be a cold luncheon for about thirty guests. I had cooked a number of chickens the day before; even some of the good, laying pullets had had to be sacrificed. The first thing I did was to prepare all the salads, which I put in the dairy to keep cool and fresh; then there was the butter to be pressed into hundreds of small pats. There was a giant veal-and-ham pie that I had made myself. It looked so real, just like something out of Mrs Beeton's. I was very proud of it, but it was rather overshadowed by the wedding-cake, which was in three layers and came from a shop.

There was the table to be laid. May and I had put five leaves in it last night and it looked simply enormous. It had to be covered by two tablecloths. In the cellar there were masses of daffodils which had been picked the day before. I brought them up and arranged them on the table and all around the room, and the bright spring sunshine came through the French window and everything looked lovely in spite of being so shabby.

That morning the whole family, including the bride, had

breakfast in the large kitchen, and when Auntie – the daily woman who did the rough – arrived, she sat down in her rusty hat like a black pudding, and had breakfast, too.

Soon after breakfast the relations started to arrive. Very old ladies were carefully unpacked from old-fashioned cars full of moths. Girl cousins came on bicycles to know if they could help. Later on, a few rather shy R.A.F. young men turned up. They didn't know what to do until the girl cousins took them in hand. While all these people were arriving, Rose had retired to her room, but soon she caused great consternation by coming downstairs wearing a ski-ing suit and a large sun hat covered by a thick veil. She said she was going to inspect the bees to see if they had survived the winter, and if they had, tell them about her wedding. Everyone followed her and tried to make her leave the bees alone, but she took no notice and went down the garden to the hives. The bees had survived the winter rather well. They were a very savage kind called British Blacks and one old lady and several members of the Air Force got stung, but fortunately the bride escaped.

Then it was time for the people to go to church, and there was just Rose and May and their father left. The girls were upstairs dressing and Mr Redhead walked up and down the hall, biting his moustache and looking rather fierce and worried. Then one of the dogs was sick in the hall as well.

When Rose came down she was looking really beautiful, and May looked very fresh and nice. She hustled Rose and her father into the car and they were gone. I ran to the dining-room to make sure all the windows and doors were shut so that the animals could not get at the banquet. They were great thieves. Often the cats and dogs would eat the entire joint before

162

humans even saw it. In spite of the dog being sick in the hall, everything was safe.

I went to the church through the fields, but did not enter, because I had no hat and, in any case, the church was too crowded. I stood in the porch with a huddle of village women. They were saying Mrs Redhead's grave should have been decorated on such a day as this, so I felt rather embarrassed.

When Rose and her husband came out there was a great shower of confetti and the local photographer took photographs. All the usual things happened, even an old shoe was tied to the car. I became carried away by the general rush and found myself returning to the house in a car with some quite nice people. I was glad I was wearing my best suit. Rose had to stand in the drawing-room when we came back. She had to keep shaking hands and receiving congratulations. I went into the kitchen to make sure the two girls we had engaged to wait at table had turned up; they had.

Everybody went into the dining-room; I wasn't sure if I was meant to attend the wedding-breakfast or just wash it up in the scullery – nobody had said anything about it – so I sat on the kitchen table and waited for someone to come out looking for me; but only the girls who waited at table came out and a lot of laughter and noise. So I went into the scullery and helped Auntie. She kept wiping her face on her sack apron and making remarks about me not being in the dining-room and that she would have thought they would have asked me and things like that. It made me sad and awkward, so I went up to my bedroom and sat looking out of the window and felt hollow and depressed. After a time there were voices and goodbyes and cars starting and I knew it was time to go downstairs and clear up.

33

It was Sandro's Easter holidays and we used to go for long walks every afternoon. Usually we went through the fields to the woods. We were quite alone there except for birds and animals. Often I would sit reading on a log while Sandro explored. Sometimes we would fish in the lake. We hadn't real rods, only home-made ones; but we had real hooks, not bent pins. Quite often we caught fish large enough to eat, but we always put them back alive. It was just the excitement of feeling them tugging on the line, and seeing the cork that served as a float bobbing up and down, that we really liked. When the fish was landed we almost wished we hadn't caught it, because it was so beastly getting the hooks out of their mouths, poor dears. I think lots of the fish in that lake must have kind of hare-lips now.

During the Christmas holidays we had learnt to skate there. I never thought I could learn to do a thing like that, and I loved it so much. I think the afternoons skating must have been the happiest I had ever had. The feel of the cold air on my face as I glided round and the exciting sound of our skates cutting the ice – suddenly a startled blackbird would fly in a great hurry from a bush, scattering hoar-frost and giving little cries. In the distance there was always someone chopping wood, which made us feel warmer somehow.

The woods were delightful all the year round. Even when it was raining there were so many trees we didn't get really wet. In the spring there were masses of primroses and bluebells, and people would come and pick them and we would see their long white stalks draped over the backs of bicycles, and often see great bunches just picked and left to die of thirst. When it was summer there would be wild raspberries, and we seemed to be the only people who bothered to pick them, and I used to make them into the most heavenly jam. There were blackberries, too. Everything that should be in a wood was there.

One afternoon I was sitting on my log, reading an Edwardian romance – almost the only kind of book on the Redheads' shelves, except for a few sporting books and some *Punches* and *Girls' Annuals*. By now I would have welcomed some of Mrs Redhead's library detective stories. I'd almost forgotten what it was like to read real books. I suddenly stopped reading, because I heard Sandro call out, and I thought, 'Oh, God! he has fallen in the water.' Then, with great relief, I saw him running towards me. His feet made no sound, because he had taken off his socks and shoes. He was carrying something in his arms that looked like a giant hedgehog. He shouted, 'Look! I've found a wild puppy,' and when he came near I saw it was a fox cub. I took it from him because I was scared it would bite, but although it was frightened, it didn't. It just crept under my jacket and hid its face.

It was a lovely little thing, grey-brown, with black legs and a nice white shirt-front, and so fat we couldn't bear to part with it. So we ran home and smuggled it into our part of the house, and I put it down in Sandro's bedroom, where it disappeared under the bed. We thought it better to leave it alone until it got used to houses, and we left it alone with a saucer of milk.

When it was time to put Sandro to bed we found it had drunk the milk and was playing with a tiny brush Sandro had had when he was a baby. It ran away as soon as we came into the room, but after he had been in bed some time, the cub jumped on the bed and, when Sandro wisely took no notice of it, began to play with him, and kept jumping on and off the bed and racing round the room. When I came to see how they were I found Sandro asleep and couldn't see the fox anywhere, then I discovered it curled up under the bedclothes. I took it away in case it had fleas and made it a little bed in a clothes-basket. I put it in our bathroom and tucked it in with one of the Redheads' hot-water bottles and a chop bone.

In the morning I found it had eaten the bone and part of the hot-water bottle as well. Several times during the night I had been wakened by the noise of sharp, hard little barks. I hoped no one else had heard it. This morning it was so friendly and pleased to see me and ran after a ball of paper I threw for it. When I went outside to feed the baby chickens that lived on the lawn I found one dead, so I gave it to Foxy to eat and he crunched it up in a minute. I was usually most distressed when the chickens died, but now I was quite glad and hoped some more would die soon.

We kept the secret of our fox for about a week, but eventually May remarked on the weird bird that seemed to haunt the garden every night. 'It might even be a fox,' she said. So I told her there was one living in the house, and she went all stiff and

166

displeased and said I must put it back where I found it or give it to her father to kill. I was so terribly sad when she said this; I had never seen her annoyed before. Then I thought maybe her heart would melt if she saw it, so asked her to come up to Sandro's bedroom with me to help catch it. When I opened the door Foxy frisked across the room to me, and when I bent down to pick him up he stood on his hind legs with excitement and made happy little noises. I threw a ball for him and he caught it and ran round the room with it in his mouth, then jumped on the bed and hid under the covers. May became quite enchanted with him, just as I had hoped, and said I could keep the fox if I never let her father know and it didn't get too smelly.

After a time we used to see Foxy looking sadly out of the window, and he would scratch the glass with his paws, and once he climbed up the curtains and tried to escape through the top of the window. We couldn't bear to see the poor little thing pining, so thought it would be a good idea to let it loose on the tennis lawn when we were quite sure Mr Redhead was busy on the farm. There was wire netting all round, so it would be quite safe. We managed to do this every day and he was so happy to be out in the fresh air again it made us feel quite guilty that we had kept him in such close confinement all this time. He used to dig up worms and beetles and eat them. The old poodle used to watch him through the wire and they became quite friendly. I tried the experiment of letting them loose together and they had terrific games.

One day Mr Redhead returned unexpectedly just when we thought he was doing something useful on the farm. Foxy and the poodle were playing and at first we didn't notice him; but there was a great bellow which nearly blew us off our feet.

'Who put that bloody fox on my tennis lawn?' We were rooted to the grass with fright and I thought, 'This is where I get the sack.' I looked round out of the side of my eyes, but saw him disappearing by the bee-hives and I hated him. I told Sandro we must put the fox back in the wood or Mr Redhead might murder him, but he cried so much, then before I knew what he was doing, picked the fox up and ran back to the house with it. So I decided the best thing would be to take the fox away when he was asleep in the night.

That evening as I was cooking a rabbit-pie, Mr Redhead came into the kitchen. I pushed it back into the oven with great damage to the pastry and slammed the oven door, which is a thing good cooks never do even when they are just about to get the sack. Mr Redhead did a lot of throat-clearing, then said, 'That is rather a jolly cub you have, Mrs Fairclough, but please do keep it away from my chickens,' and when I turned round to thank him, he was gone.

I ran upstairs and told Sandro Foxy was reprieved, and we danced round his bedroom and had quite a celebration.

After that the fox didn't have to be a secret one any more, and we used to take him for walks with us on a lead. Sometimes when we met people in the fields they would say, 'Isn't that dog like a fox?'

34

I was sitting on the kitchen window-sill peeling apples. Sandro came running through the garden and climbed through the window and sat on the sill, too, and he ate the apple-peel. In between his munching, he said, 'When I was playing by the lake this morning' (munch munch) 'I met a man painting, and he is putting me in his picture.' (Munch munch.) 'I was picking some large stones to make a house with, and he asked me to stay like that, picking stones,' (munch) 'so I did and now I've come in his picture.' (Munch.)

I was so startled that I cut my finger, and as I was licking the blood I thought, 'Perhaps it's Charles he has seen, or one of his friends. He will come here and remind me of things and make trouble of some sort, borrow money from the Redheads or disgrace me in the village.' I asked Sandro what he looked like, this beastly artist. Sandro said he couldn't remember, but 'He's awfully nice. You would like him, Mummy.'

The next morning he wanted to meet this wretched artist again and I refused to let him go, but he kept looking at me so reproachfully and saying, 'He was depending on me,' in such a grieving voice, I had to let him go.

I felt depressed and worried all the morning, and to make things worse, Auntie hadn't come and there was much more work than usual to do. About every six weeks or so Auntie used to take a day off, and when she returned to work she would groan and moan and say she had had measles in the throat, or a fidget in the knee – once she had a gastric foot – but I really think she used to go by bus to Bedford to see her married daughter.

At lunch Sandro was full of his new friend. He said he was called Rollo. So it wasn't Charles, after all, but maybe it was a friend of his, which was almost as bad. But I did not feel quite so depressed, and after I'd washed the luncheon things and tidied the kitchen, we put Foxy on his lead and went for a walk. It was a perfect spring day and I thought we would pick bluebells and send them to my sister Ann. We walked through the fields that led to the woods and the poodle forgot its great age and ran about stirring up the cows, and Foxy pulled and tugged this way and that until I was almost running and became entangled round the long legs of a man coming towards us. Sandro started to laugh and said, 'Here is Rollo. Now you can see how nice he is.' I was still trying to free Foxy's lead, and when I knew whose legs he was all mixed up with I dared not look up, but he bent down to help and soon was free. I had an impression of a young face with thick grey hair. I couldn't remember seeing anyone like that while I was married to Charles, so I felt much better and stood up like a normal person and said I was sorry to have got him all tangled up like that. I saw he was a terribly handsome person in spite of having grey hair. He had a delightful voice, too, and he thanked me for lending him Sandro and said he hoped I would come and see the painting. He had taken a furnished cottage by the church and the next thing that happened was we were walking to the cottage to see the painting right away.

I was rather scared and didn't say much; but he talked away in his nice voice and seemed to be charmed with Foxy; but when we arrived at the cottage Foxy became all nervous and wet the carpet, which I hoped Rollo didn't notice, then ran up the chimney and stayed there rather a long time. I sadly called 'Foxy, Foxy' up the chimney, but he didn't return. Rollo even put a piece of raw steak in the grate, but no one came down to eat it. With great firmness I restrained Sandro from climbing up the chimney after him and tried to forget Foxy and make polite conversation. The cottage was rather dark and overcrowded, but nice and peaceful, rather like a restful Sunday afternoon, which was how one would expect it to be, because it belonged to an old lady with a pug. I had often seen them doing a little gentle weeding in the garden, but I had never been inside before. Rollo said he was terrified of getting paint about or breaking something. Fortunately, a woman from the village used to come in the morning and do some cooking and cleaning. While he was telling me this Foxy suddenly appeared and ran across the carpet leaving a trail of soot and kind of grinning. I almost hated him. Rollo caught him and his beautiful light grey suit was made all sooty and Foxy tried to bite his hand. I don't think he liked men.

Rollo shut him in a cupboard where brushes lived. Then we couldn't open the door to get one to clean the carpet in case he escaped, and he said he would do it when we had gone. I couldn't help feeling he would be awfully glad when we left him in peace and safety, although he was very charming about all the disgraceful things we had caused to happen.

He showed me the painting which was almost finished and it was a strong vigorous kind of painting, full of light and colour. I could see he had used his palette knife frequently and it was most effective. I was surprised when he told me he had not done much landscape painting before, but had felt his work was growing dreary and stale and it would do him good to work in the country for a time. He mostly painted portraits and seemed to be quite successful.

While we were looking at the painting a vase of daffodils on the window-sill upset and the water started to splash on to a lovely old spinet. We looked at the window and there was an awful old brown mat trying to get in. I'd quite forgotten the poodle, and there she was, so I let her in through the door and she ran round welcoming us and caused a great disturbance. Rollo went and got a cloth to dry the spinet. When he had mopped up the water he asked us to stay to tea, but I rather felt we had outstayed our welcome and took the dirty fox out of the cupboard which he'd made a bit smelly and left quite quickly.

On the way home I let Foxy walk through the long grass to get clean, although I expect they were saving it up for hay. I felt sad; the animals had behaved so badly. Clouds had come in the sky and were going about very fast. They went over the sun so quickly the light was changing all the time and rolling shadows came across the fields and sunlight was sliding about all over the hills. When we came home I went upstairs and sat by the looking glass and looked at myself to see what had happened to my face since I'd been living with the Redheads. In a way it had improved. My skin was very clear and my eyes large and bright;

but there were some lines round my mouth and eyes that didn't use to be there; at least, I couldn't remember them. My hair was still dark and curly. It only grew as far as my shoulders, so I never had it cut. In my ears were the little gold rings I always wore to stop the holes filling up. My clothes were dull, a washed-out cellular blue shirt, a rust-coloured Shetland jumper with darns on the elbows, and an old tweed skirt I'd made from one of Rose's cast-offs. I stood regretting very much I wasn't glamorous. Then I went down and got tea.

35

For three days it rained and I spent my spare time making a blue-spotted summer frock with stiff, white muslin, puffed sleeves. I was determined not to wait till May was out before I wore it, because it really suited me very well indeed.

Sandro hadn't been able to meet Rollo since the animals disgraced themselves. It had been much too dark and wet for landscape-painting, then as soon as the weather changed he had to return to school; but if Rollo wanted to finish the painting he could always do it on a fine weekend. We had not heard anything about him lately and I began to wonder if he had returned to London already.

The first of May came and it was so warm and sunny my bedroom was simply stiff with sun as soon as I woke up, and I thought, 'I'll wear my new frock this afternoon.' Everyone seemed to be happy now the sun had come back. May came in to the kitchen and asked me to make a chocolate cake because some people were coming to tea, and I was glad, because since Rose had gone she was too much alone and worked frightfully hard on the farm and had no pleasures at all. This morning she washed her golden hair and let it dry in the sun while she mowed the lawn for the first time that year, and I opened the kitchen window to smell the new-cut grass.

Mr Redhead came into the kitchen with a great bundle of rhubarb in his arms. He said he wanted me to make it into jam – he was mad on rhubarb jam. I saw my afternoon in the sun disappearing, so I said I couldn't make it to-day, because we had no lemons in the house, but he said, 'You must make it to-day while the rhubarb is fresh; it makes all the difference. Let me see, I seem to remember seeing one in the kitchen this morning when I made my early tea,' and he started looking around. I knew where several lemons were, but I didn't say anything. He looked towards the dresser, which was usually rather loaded with odds and ends. 'Ah! there it is,' and he pounced on a lemon mixed up with the eggs on the rack and put it on the great mound of rhubarb with triumph, and I had to pretend I thought he was awfully clever, although I wanted to throw the lemon at his fussy face and burn the rhubarb on the range. I was glad when I returned to the kitchen after going upstairs to make the beds to see the pile of rhubarb had dwindled away considerably. Auntie was very fond of it.

Although it was such a warm day I had to cook a great, stuffy lunch of greasy mutton and roast potatoes – even with the window open the kitchen became stifling. Then, after lunch, there was all the sordid washing up to face, and when that was finished there was the wretched jam. I lit the oil stove, because jam always burnt if we made it on the range. It smelt awful; it always did. I prepared the rhubarb and cut it up into small pieces, and put it in the large brass pan, and after a time a great smell of hot jam joined the other smells. I stood over the oil stove, stirring away and every now and then trying it in a saucer to see if it would set. A cuckoo flew over the house and settled in a tree. Then I heard the yard dog barking and saw the cowman fetch the cows from the field and knew it must be milking time and the afternoon nearly over. The door-bell rang and May went and welcomed her friends. There was a lot of talk in the hall and I heard her say, 'We will have tea in the garden.' Then there were sounds of deck chairs being taken out. I put the tea-things on a tray. The scones and chocolate cake I'd made that morning looked delicious. I left it all ready for May to fetch. They usually got their own tea. I went back to my jam-stirring. The visitors seemed to be coming into the kitchen to help May carry the tea-things. I felt ashamed for them to see me all hot and sticky; there was even jam on my ears, and I'd cried a bit and gone all blotchy.

The visitors came into the kitchen. Out of the corner of my eye I saw a girl in a fresh linen dress. I knew her slightly, because she came quite often to the house, usually on a horse, and once she had ridden it right into the kitchen and it had eaten the apples I'd put in a dish all ready to bake, and I had to lead it round the table to get it the right way for going out of the door again. She didn't have a horse with her, but a man. I didn't look at him, but when I heard him say, 'Let me carry that tray, Miss Redhead,' I knew it was Rollo. When he saw me bent over the disgusting jam, he said, 'Good afternoon. How are you?' and the girls seemed surprised he knew me. I hunched myself up and murmured, 'I'm feeling beastly, thank you,' and great puffs of jammy steam came in my face. May said, 'That jam smells as if it's burning.' Then they went out of the kitchen. She was quite right. When I emptied the jam into the jars the bottom of the brass pan was all burnt and I had to spend about an hour cleaning it.

When Sandro came home from school he saw the tea-party on the lawn, and when he recognised Rollo he wanted to climb out of the window to speak to him, but I wouldn't let him. We had our tea on a tray by the back door. I couldn't bear to see that tea-party and I felt terribly tired of being a cook.

After tea I remembered Foxy had not been out all day. He had been shut in the bathroom all the afternoon and had scratched the door rather badly and made a mess. We took him down to the willow brook and Sandro played houses in the split old willow trees. Some were all black inside because they had been struck by lightning, but they were still alive. Foxy skipped around breaking down the tender young nettles, which smelt delightful, and we both forgot we had been prisoners all day.

The following morning there was a letter for me – a thing which seldom happened. It had a local postmark and was addressed in rather square writing. I didn't open it for several hours, because I liked to think it was something exciting and knew it would turn into a letter from Sandro's school saying he must bring a pair of slippers to school if I opened it; but as long as it remained unopened it could be an invitation to a dance or a letter from an unknown admirer or something impossible. When I opened the letter it didn't turn into something dreary, after all. It was a heavenly note from Rollo asking me which evening I would be free to have dinner with him at Bentley Hall – a hotel about four miles away.

Bentley Hall was really a kind of road-house on the golf course, very bogus and imitation antique, but the only place of that sort for miles. Rose used to go there quite often and I used to envy her, and when I had to pass that way I always walked slowly to see all the rich, care-free people coming in and out. They had beautiful cars and trimmed poodles, and they always seemed to be young and good-looking; but once I heard two elegant people sitting in an open cream car talking, and the man was moaning about his overdraft and the woman seemed pretty miserable, too, and I was almost glad. Now I was going to go there, too. I wondered how we would get there, because Rollo didn't appear to have a car.

I asked May which evening I could have free, and she seemed quite startled, but said I could have the following Friday, so I wrote to Rollo and said I would be free on Friday evening. I looked at my clothes, and the only fresh-looking dress was the spotted one; but it didn't look the sort of thing they would wear at Bentley Hall. In my tin cash-box there was eleven pounds seven and six. It had taken me three years to save that in case I got the sack and we had nowhere to go. I became overcome with temptation, and the next day caught the bus to Bedford. I had to do it in the afternoon and would only get about an hour there, but I knew exactly what I wanted. In that hour I found just the kind of dress I was looking for. It was real silk and had a most elegantly shaped bodice and a pleated skirt. It cost nine guineas. There was just enough money left to buy a pair of delicate sandals and some real silk stockings, so I bought them at a shop nearby. Then it was time to catch my bus home. I felt rather shy of bumping into the Redheads with my grand looking parcels. I managed to get into the house without meeting them and found Sandro sadly waiting for his tea in the kitchen. I felt very guilty when I saw him and remembered I'd spent all our money and hadn't even bought him a toy, so I gave him a shilling to buy some sweets with; but I still felt guilty and could see ruin staring us in the face, but that wore off when it was time to go to bed and I went upstairs and tried all my new clothes on and the frock fitted perfectly, and the sandals were so light and dainty; even in the speckled, old looking glass I looked almost beautiful and I was glad I'd spent all our money.

Rollo 'phoned on Friday morning to say he would fetch me at seven o'clock. I was glad I'd answered the 'phone myself because I was shy for the Redheads to know I was having dinner with Rollo. I knew May would be so surprised if she knew.

It was a heavenly day and I kept running outside to make sure there weren't any clouds. If it was raining or cold, my new clothes would look so unsuitable. I knew it was dangerous to be too happy, because something always goes wrong, but I just couldn't help being happy that day. I even felt I loved Auntie, and let her drink a bottle of Mr Redhead's beer at lunch.

In the afternoon I went to the woods with Foxy and lay in the sun, which came in an opening between the trees. Through my half-closed eyes I watched Foxy playing and digging small holes. A large fly came on my leg. I saw it had strange red eyes and a blue body. I'd always thought they were black before, but now I knew they were quite beautiful.

The dreamy, happy day passed and at last it was time to put Sandro to bed, and then it was time to put on my new clothes. I had a bath and dressed very slowly, and before I put my dress on I gave my hair a great brushing. At last I was ready, and I felt so pleased with my reflection I just stood in front of the looking glass. It was the first time I'd worn a really lovely dress.

Just as I was rolling a lipstick and powder-puff in a hanky so that I needn't take my shabby bag with me, I heard May calling. I ran downstairs and when I reached the kitchen there was May coming in, still calling me. She looked rather red and put out. She said, 'There is a friend of yours in the drawing-room.' She gave a bewildered glance at my clothes, but before she could say anything else I hurried away. I felt scared to go into the drawing-room. I could hear Rollo and Mr Redhead talking. Mr Redhead would wonder what on earth I was doing, marching into the drawing-room and snaffling his guest away. When I put my nose round the door they were drinking sherry. Then Mr Redhead said, 'Yes, Mrs Fairclough, what do you want?' So Rollo explained I was having dinner with him, but it took some time for Mr Redhead to understand. Then he said, 'Why go out to dinner? Stay here. I'm sure my daughter would be delighted to have you. She is lonely since Rose married.' I felt pretty awful. It would have been so lovely if I'd been given a glass of sherry and Mr Redhead had forgotten I was a cook for a few minutes. But eventually Rollo got me out of the house and into the car, which he said he had borrowed from the girl friend who had a horse. I would have rather walked than used her car and I began to feel, 'All this is the result of being too happy all day.' Rollo talked away in his delightful voice, but I said nothing. I felt everything was going to be a disappointment, and hadn't the heart to talk.

When we reached Bentley Hall there were masses of cars outside and I began to feel more cheerful. We went inside and sat in a large lounge with beams and stags' heads all over the place; but it was very comfortable and there were bowls and bowls of tulips all around. A waiter brought some cocktails. I wasn't sure if you eat the cherry or not – it was such a long time since I'd had one. Rollo ate his, so I did, too. I became happy again, but was too shy to say much. I just listened to Rollo talking, and sometimes asked him questions.

I asked how he had discovered this village, and he said the people who lent him the car this evening were old friends of his and had taken the cottage by the church for him. I was happy to hear him say he expected to be there for at least another month. I couldn't bear to think of him going away for ever. He told me his father was an architect; at least, had been one until recently. He was dead now, and his mother was dead, too. He told me about his father's house in St John's Wood. It was rather large and had a garden full of apple and pear trees and flowering cherry trees, too. It was beautiful in the spring with all the blossom, not like being in London at all. He didn't live in the house himself, because he already had a studio, but was thinking of letting it furnished until he had made up his mind what to do with it. He thought there were toy railways and all kinds of things in one of the attics that he had when he was a boy and he promised he would hunt them out and give them to Sandro.

Then we went into the dining-room and had a heavenly dinner, the first time I had eaten a meal that I hadn't cooked myself for over three years. We drank wine and I began to talk. I didn't feel shy any more and an awful lot of words came pouring out. I told him about my married life with Charles and a little about Peregrine – but I didn't mention Fanny; and I told him about Ann and my brother, and our life in the country when my parents were alive, and the batty old governesses we used to have before we went to boarding-school, and the three deaf white cats I used to have – they all had odd eyes, one yellow and one blue – and about my father eating a wasp in the jam when we were having tea in the garden under the trees, and how he swallowed the wasp and it stung him as it went down and he was dead in twenty-four hours. I told him a lot of things and he seemed to be interested. It was such a relief to talk to a real person, not just the people I worked for. I was always afraid of upsetting them and making them think I wasn't a suitable person to have in the house.

We went back to the lounge and stags and coffee. Everyone looked at us when we came into the room, because Rollo was so tall and handsome, and I felt so proud to be with such a distinguished man. He was wearing a beautiful silver-grey suit with rather high lapels, and it suited him well. While we were having coffee, Rollo said he had met Charles about a year ago and had actually visited his studio. He said he thought his paintings very good, but they varied a lot. He was always trying new methods of painting and destroying his previous work. He believed he had gone to live in Paris now; but what really interested me was that he said Charles had a prehistoric-looking object in a bowl of water and it sounded as if he had kept Great Warty all these years and my heart quite warmed to Charles.

After our coffee we walked in the gardens, which looked more interesting than they really were in the half light. There were still people bathing, and their voices echoed and were strange. There was an early owl sitting on a fence. We walked carefully until we could almost touch it; it was still too light for it to be able to see us, and we looked into its puss-like face before it flew away on moth wings. We went to the bathing-pool. Someone had recently dived and the board was still quivering. The bathers looked queerly beautiful in the dim light and dark water, but made us feel cold, so we wandered back to the garden, and Rollo held my arm and I was glad my dress had short sleeves so that I could feel his hand against my arm.

It was time to go home, because the Redheads always went to bed early and I would have to ring the bell and bring Mr Redhead down in his nightshirt if I was late. So Rollo drove me home and we were back so soon, but the house was all locked up. Rollo tried all the doors with me. None of them would open. He wanted to ring the bell, but I was terrified of the idea of Mr Redhead snarling in his nightshirt. We went to the back of the house again. Then I remembered there were some ladders in the yard and we fetched one and it just reached my window, and I started to go up the ladder, but Rollo called me down. He said he wanted to paint a portrait of me and could I start sitting for it to-morrow, and I said I would come to the cottage to-morrow afternoon. Then he kissed me good night and I don't know how I got up the ladder after that, but I did, and he took it and put it back in the yard, and the Redheads knew nothing about it.

The next morning May asked me how I had enjoyed myself, and I told her I had had a heavenly evening, and she asked me how I had met Rollo, so I told her about him painting Sandro and that he was starting a portrait of me this afternoon. I could see she was longing to ask about the new clothes, but didn't know quite how to put it, and while she was hesitating I started talking about the day's meals and ginger puddings and things like that.

I hardly knew how I did my work that day. I only discovered

just in time that I was putting Keating's Powder in the pudding instead of ginger; but somehow the morning passed and the lunch was eaten and washed up. As soon as my duties were over I tore upstairs and changed my clothes and hurried down the fields. I could feel the Redheads shaking their heads over me.

When I arrived at the cottage the door was open, so I went straight in. It gave me a lovely feeling to be so intimate with Rollo. He was in the kitchen priming a canvas and looking rather worried. He said, 'Darling, however am I going to paint you in this tiny cottage?' We hadn't thought of that. All the rooms were minute. Eventually, he decided to paint me in the garden. I was a bit scared of this idea, in case any of the village people passed and saw me on their way to the church.

He painted me lying on the grass in the sun, which suited me very well, because I loved to be in the sun and hoped the village people couldn't see me unless they came and peered right over the hedge, but forgot they could see Rollo standing in front of his easel, and after a time there was quite a row of heads wearing various frightful hats bobbing over the hedge. So we thought it was time to go in and have an early tea and I got it ready while Rollo washed his brushes.

We had tea in the sitting-room, and it was a relief there were no animals this time. When we had finished our tea, Rollo came and sat beside me on the old-fashioned sofa, and I hoped he would make love to me; but when he did I felt all shaky and kind of worried. When he asked me to marry him, I didn't like to answer in case it was a mistake and he hadn't really said it; but he asked me again, so I knew it was real. I looked at him and thought what a marvellous husband he would be. He would never eat children's birthday cakes before they saw them, or take the money out of their money-boxes; but even if he did I would still love him and think him wonderful. Then I told him about Fanny and all about Peregrine and his disgusting wife, and any odds and ends of awful things I could remember doing. He heard them all, but it only seemed to make him love me even more. We became engaged to be married.

37

The Redheads stopped shaking their heads over me when I became engaged, and I had letters of congratulation from Ann and my brother. My brother's letter was very pompous, but Ann asked if I would like to spend a weekend with her in London. I told Rollo about this invitation and he thought it would be a good idea. He could come to London at the same time and show me his father's house. Then I could see if I would like to live there when we were married.

I asked the Redheads if I could go away for the weekend, and May was most helpful and offered to look after Sandro while I was away, because it would be rather a squash for us both to stay at Ann's flat; in any case, I don't think he was included in Ann's invitation.

We went on this London visit the first weekend in June and we travelled together in the train. It was wonderful to be coming back to London after three years, and when we arrived I refused to use a taxi. I was so longing to go in a red bus again. We went straight to Ann's flat and I could see Rollo made a great impression on her. She gave us some sherry and there was a great deal of talking. Then Rollo 'phoned Prunier's and reserved a table for dinner. I enjoyed that dinner so much, and I still have a box of book matches in the shape of fish that I took home that evening.

On Sunday we went to see Rollo's house in St John's Wood. I would have preferred to have gone without Ann, but she had been so kind about my engagement I had to ask her to come, too. Rollo looked a little disappointed when he called for me in a taxi and discovered she was coming as well; but she enjoyed exploring the house so much we were quite glad we had brought her afterwards. It was a delightful house – early Victorian, with a high-walled garden. The blossom was over, but there were masses of roses just coming out and the flowerbeds were filled with tree-lupins in the most beautiful colours. Against the house there was a grape-vine. I couldn't believe I could be queen of all this. I said, 'Oh, Rollo, please let's live in this heavenly house. Don't let it to anyone. We must keep it ourselves.' He laughed, because I hadn't even been in the house yet, but I knew I would love it and I did. All the rooms on the hall floor had three large windows that opened inwards, and they had small iron balconies. The house seemed filled with sun and air. The kitchens were semi-basement, but were large and homely, with great cupboards and dressers let in the walls, and the floors were made of red tiles. There were three large bedrooms and a small dressing-room upstairs and the most wonderful modern bathroom that his father had put in quite recently. There was another narrow flight of stairs that led to the attics, but only the maid's bedroom was furnished; but one room was simply stiff with lovely, old-fashioned toys, a snorting rocking-horse and a huge Noah's Ark filled with beautifully made animals, not beastly flat animals like they have in modern arks. I couldn't bear to leave the toys, but there was so much to see. Most of the rooms were furnished with very beautiful antique furniture, and there were some elegant Georgian mirrors on the walls; but the pictures were mostly rather heavy and dark with the exception of the ones Rollo had painted himself. We decided to scrap all the old paintings, and some of the curtains were a bit fussy. We thought it would be a good idea to repaint and distemper the whole house, so Rollo wrote down in a notebook all the things we thought wanted doing to the house.

Then Rollo rang the old-fashioned bell in the drawing-room and the maid, who had been acting as caretaker since his father died, came. I had already met her in the kitchen. Rollo told her to bring some sherry, and it came like magic on a heavy silver tray, and I thought that when I was married I could ring that bell.

The weekend passed so quickly; but it didn't matter much, because it was only a foretaste of the happiness that was coming when I married. When I returned to the farm I used to lie awake at night thinking of our beautiful house and the cupboards stacked with china dinner-services and tea-sets, and elegant glasses for every kind of drink. There was a great linen cupboard all warm and stiff with real linen, and the eiderdowns had been put away in muslin bags to keep them clean. I hoped the Redheads would come and see me when I was married. I was leaving them in three weeks' time and a grim woman with a knobby face was coming to take my place. They said they were scared of her.

Rose came to stay for a few days before she went abroad. Her husband brought her down by car, but he didn't stay, and I think

189

May was glad to have her on her own so that she could spoil her. She was going to have a baby already, and she was delighted, because it gave her a really good excuse to be lazy, and she lay about eating sweets all day and looked very charming. She didn't even stir up the bees. May bought some baby wool and tried to interest her in knitting small garments, but she said as she had all the bother of making the baby someone else could make the clothes.

There was one thing that cast rather a blight on my marriage. Rollo didn't want Foxy to live with us for some reason. He would have been so happy in St John's Wood. He could have had one of the attic bedrooms and that lovely garden to play in, but Rollo was adamant about not having him; perhaps because he had made a mess in the broom cupboard, and once by the willow brook he had bitten his leg, but not very badly. I hoped he would relent right until my last day at the Redheads'. He had returned to London, so I sent him a telegram asking if he was sure he didn't want Foxy, but he replied, 'Quite sure.' Men are much firmer than women. On my last evening, Sandro and I went down to the woods with Foxy and let him play by us and when he wasn't looking we just went away. In the night I heard him barking in the garden and went out to him in my nighty and he jumped up into my arms, so I took him back and had him in my bed all night. But early in the morning I took him a long way away, several miles. I carried him all the way. There was a heavy dew and all the birds were singing. When we came to the place where they reared pheasants I put him down, and I put a large piece of the Redheads' joint beside him, but he wasn't interested; he kept skipping about and sniffing the birds and quite forgot me, so I went away and felt too sad to cry. I felt guilty like the father in Hansel and Gretel.

I felt kind of sorry when I said goodbye to the Redheads after breakfast. It wasn't like parting with Foxy, but they had been very kind really, and the years there hadn't been too unhappy, just dull and lonely. I said goodbye to Auntie and caught her in the act of hiding some bacon in her petticoat, but we didn't mention it. Then one of the farm men took us to the station in the milk float and I wasn't a cook any more. Those days were over for ever.

I took Sandro to stay with my brother and his wife, because we couldn't very well take him on our honeymoon. He didn't like being left there much at first. Then he discovered a stream at the end of the garden and he started to make a boat out of a log and hardly noticed me going. Then I went to London and Rollo met me at the station and he looked so happy and pleased to see me it didn't seem so bad about parting with Foxy. We had lunch together and he told me he had made arrangements for us to go to Portugal for our honeymoon. Everything had become so wonderful. He loved to surprise me with thrilling things we were going to do. I'd hardly got over the excitement about Portugal when he suggested we went to buy a trousseau, and directly we left the restaurant we did, and we went on buying it for three days. Then we had to buy some trunks to put it in.

We were married in a register office. Ann and a friend of Rollo's called Simon were witnesses, and after the wedding we had an enormous lunch at Boulestin's. We drank a lot of wine and felt quite dazed when we came out into the hot sunshine. We said goodbye to the witnesses and took a taxi to St John's Wood. We sat in the garden drinking tea under the apple trees and I said it would be nice to have a goldfish pond, and Rollo went into the house quite suddenly, and I felt lonely and worried in case I'd said something to distress him. Perhaps his mother had been drowned in a goldfish pond at some time. When he returned he told me he had been telephoning a landscape gardener, and when we came home there would be a goldfish pond complete with fish, and if there was anything else I would have done to the garden that would be done as well.

The day after we were married we got up very early and flew to Lisbon. It seemed years ago I'd been driven to the station in the milk float. Before we left the house in St John's Wood I went into every room so that I could remember how beautiful it was while I was away, and I went into the garden and marked the place where I wanted the pond made. I didn't want any other alterations, because it was all so perfect.

THE LAST CHAPTER

This is the end of my book, but not the end of my story, which will go on until I die; but now we have come to such a happy part of my life there is very little to say about it. At first, because I wasn't used to happiness and freedom from worry, I would be terrified that disaster was coming round the corner at any minute. I expected that Rollo would suddenly say he didn't love me any more, or that the house was mortgaged up to the hilt and we must sell everything we had got and go and live in one room, and almost every time he went out without me I thought the telephone would ring to say he had been run over, and if he caught cold I believed it was the end and he was going to develop pneumonia and die. When none of these things happened I worried about Sandro, but there was nothing wrong there either, so gradually I ceased to imagine all the dreadful things that might happen.

Although Rollo was rather grave and quiet, he had a number of friends, and most of them became mine, too. We used to entertain quite a lot and I became rather famous as a cook, so my time at the Redheads' wasn't altogether wasted. It was lovely to cook and know someone else would tidy up all the mess and wash up. One of Rollo's friends, called Simon, became engaged to Ann, so the perfect bachelor girl was no more, but perhaps she would turn into the perfect wife.

Once rather a nasty shadow from the past crept near me like a dark spider, but it vanished again. It was at the private view of an exhibition of Rollo's paintings, and I was feeling so proud of him. I walked about among the people to hear all the nice things they were saying about his paintings. Across the gallery I saw a girl called Helen. I was very fond of her and hurried over, and she was laughing at me struggling through the people. Just as I reached her I noticed someone looking very intently at a painting of me with a lap full of large shells and I didn't speak to Helen; I just looked at that man – it was Peregrine. He looked all gruesome, very yellow, thin and bitter. I turned away quickly before he could see me, and there was Helen looking so surprised, and I said, 'Come away.' We went to a small room at the back of the gallery. There were some drinks there to jolly customers along when they were making up their mind to buy a painting. We had a drink and sat there for a little time. Then I sent Helen back to see if the man with the disagreeable yellow face was still there; but he had gone.

The exhibition was a great success and almost every painting was sold and Rollo received a number of commissions. One of them was to paint an elderly general who was about to die any minute. Rollo had to go to the country to paint this portrait. It was the first time we had been parted and I missed him so much. The house and all my treasures seemed nothing without him, and in our bedroom in the wardrobe all his suits were

194

waiting for him. Everything seemed to be still and waiting for his return; even the bathwater seemed to come out of the taps all hushed.

I 'phoned Helen and asked her to keep me company. I told her about the waiting suits and hushed taps, so she came straight away. I took her into the garden to show her the pond. The goldfish had had some black children. Then she saw the bicycle I used to use when I lived in the country. Now Sandro used to ride it in the garden although it was much too large. As soon as she saw it she wanted to ride. She had no idea how people rode bicycles, but she would keep trying, and I had to run up and down the garden pushing her. It became very warm, but although she kept falling off she would persevere. I was delighted when the brake became bent and prevented the wheels going round any more. Then we sat peacefully in the sun until the maid came out to tell us lunch was ready.

We brought our coffee into the garden. We would have liked to have eaten our lunch in the garden, too, but I thought the maid wouldn't approve. Once when she had an evening out she had come back early and discovered Rollo and me eating in the kitchen. She had looked quite hurt. She didn't really like me to do any cooking, so I only did it when we had people to dinner; but she was a dear old thing and it was marvellous having her.

We sat in the sun and drank our coffee. It was very strong and sweet. Helen talked about her husband, who was called Harold, and I looked at disturbed ants who were dashing about with large eggs. Suddenly she stopped talking about Harold and said, 'Was that sinister man your ex-husband?' For a moment I didn't answer. Then I told her about Peregrine. It was a waste to talk about such distressing subjects on such a lovely spring afternoon, but she listened and I talked on and on and the ants carrying their eggs walked over our bare legs and we hardly noticed, and that is really how I came to write this story.

virago

To buy any of our books and to find out more
about Virago Press and Virago Modern Classics,
our authors and titles, as well as events and
book club forum, visit our websites

www.virago.co.uk
www.littlebrown.co.uk

and follow us on Twitter

@ViragoBooks

To order any Virago titles p & p free in the UK,
please contact our mail order supplier on:

+ 44 (0)1832 737525

Customers not based in the UK should contact
the same number for appropriate postage
and packing costs.